Hannah

Kate Petty was born in 1951, the youngest
of four children. Her own teenage years were
spent at a coeducational boarding-school,
before going on to York University. She
divides her working life between publishing
and writing. She lives in London with her
husband and teenage son and daughter.

Hannah

KATE PETTY

Dolphin Paperbacks

These books are for Rachel, who approved

When Sophie rang and asked if I'd like to come to a sleepover on their last night of term I was really pleased. Sophie, Charlotte and Maddy are still my best friends even though I go to a different school from them now. My terms are shorter, so I'd already been vegging out for a few days. I wouldn't say I was bored exactly, just in need of a better class of company than my nerdy older brother Jeremy can provide.

My parents are awesomely high-powered. Dad is a barrister and Mum is a financial consultant. You'd think they'd enjoy a bit of high-powered leisure as well, but they both seem to find their work endlessly fascinating. Holiday is a word that barely features in their joint vocabulary. Actually they don't have a joint vocabulary. They don't really choose to spend a lot of time together, which might explain why jolly family outings don't appeal. As far as they're concerned, holidays are time out from school when J and I are expected to brush up on subjects extracurricular. So it's music courses for me – I play the flute – and genius stuff like astrophysics for J. He's heading for

Oxford and I'm expected to excel in one way or another. All very stressful.

So. I made the most of my extra week's holiday (before the parents complain that I don't get up until lunchtime), and I felt nicely de-stressed, but the other three were still high as kites from their last day of term.

Maddy and Charlotte were already there when I arrived. Maddy's a laugh. She'll be on the telly one day, that girl. She's absolutely stunningly beautiful, everything I'm not, with a lovely figure, a terrific tan, honey-gold hair and black eyelashes. Makes you sick really. She wears expensive scent and she's very touchy-feely. Loads of kisses all round. She speaks in italics – 'Hi, Hannah. How *are* you? You look *amazing*. You *do*. Really.' You know the sort of thing. Not an enormous brain, but you can't help liking her.

Now Charlotte I'm very fond of. She's your original sweet girl. Smallish, mousey hair, big blue eyes, very shy and self-conscious, but really nice. Her self-esteem is zilch, which I blame on her brassy older sister myself. Perhaps she'll come into her own when her sister leaves home. She blushes a lot, which she hates because it makes it so easy for people to tease her.

We were all in Sophie's loft. It's typical of Sophie that she even has a loft. She's tall and cool and things seem to work for her. Her older brother Danny is very straight, but not half such a geek as J, and her parents always seem pleasantly chaotic and easygoing. Unlike mine. It would be easy to be jealous of Sophie, and sometimes I am. It's not as if she has more material things than I do, just an enviable home life. But she's a good friend and always has been.

Sophie's mum lays on great food, and they had set out mattresses round the TV so we could all watch a video later. Charlotte was feeding her face. Maddy was regaling Sophie with tales of their maths teacher. Maddy reckons he's got a crush on her – he probably has. I went and sat with Charlotte and the dips. 'Hi Hannah. Save me from eating all this stuff. I'm fat enough as it is!' (See what I mean?) I laid into the doritos and guacamole.

'Now you lot have finished term I feel the holidays have really begun,' I told her. 'It's not the same when everyone else is still at school. You're not going to the Lake District straight away, are you?'

'I've got a few days to get ready, thank God.'

'Me too.' I was going to savour these next few days.

Maddy was turning through the videos. 'Shall I set the vid going now? Are we all here, Soph?' she asked. Typical Mads. Can't she count to four?

'No, let's wait for my brother to go out first,' said Sophie. So we were treated to a Maddy and Sophie dance special instead. I still can't figure out how they know what to do – just watch endless videos, I suppose. I'm a radio person myself. I'm more interested in what's new than what's popular.

Dan went out with a slam of the front door and we had the house to ourselves soon after that. So then the fun and games could begin. We let the video roll while some of us concentrated on eating and others on drinking. My posh schoolfriends (i.e. not Sophie, Maddy and Charlotte) are all spoilt brats, and drinking's a big thing with them – those that haven't expanded their minds still further with other stuff. I suppose you could say that I'm finding out about alcohol, but not in a big way, honest. I've decided that I like red wine better than white wine because the parents always offer me wine with dinner (when they're there), very French, don't you know. Gin's nice with lots of tonic, but it makes you drunk; vodka doesn't taste of anything – so I don't see the point – but it doesn't give you a headache; and whisky's plain horrible. My schoolfriends like Bailey's and other sticky drinks, but I think they're a waste of money. So sophisticated, aren't I? Anyway, I'd nabbed a bottle of Dad's Law Society wine – he buys it by the case – and we shared it out. There was some cider too, but I do know *not to mix my drinks.*

I don't remember much about the food – or the video, because it was some horror thing I'd already seen a million times. Good special effects, though. I'd love to watch them making some of these things. But as far as I'm concerned, the best bit of a sleepover comes next, once we're all in our nightclothes. Maddy wears tons of make-up, not that she needs to, and spends hours with cleansers and toners and face packs and stuff getting it off, so we usually muck about with it too. Mum wears minimal make-up (and of course she's far to busy to chat with her only daughter about such things) and we practically get expelled if we wear it for school, so I'm not much good with it. Also I'm dark, so my eyebrows and eyelashes are dark already – not that you can see much behind my specs. But Maddy decided to give me a makeover once I'd taken my glasses off for the night. Eyeshadow, eyeliner, mascara and blushers and lipstick. I looked quite good actually. Perhaps there's hope for me yet! I kept it on because the others wanted to turn the lights out and talk about guess what.

All-girls school plus a brother who doesn't seem to understand the essential difference between boys and girls means that my hands-on (so to speak) experience of the opposite sex is pretty flimsy. So I just keep quiet when they're talking about the boys in their year. Maddy's been out with loads of boys. Sophie and Charlotte go to the same parties as she does, so I'd guess that a certain amount of hands-on experience is exactly what they have had. The name Ben Southwell cropped up rather frequently with the fascinating fact that 'he kisses like a fish'. Obviously I wasn't missing much! But then they got on to Leonardo di Caprio and Brad Pitt. Well, they're OK, but sadly for me all my favourite men are dead. I mean, how can you improve on Louis Armstrong – or John Lennon, or even Kurt Cobain? Perhaps it's time I got a

5

little more realistic. I'm sure I could find someone who looked like John Lennon.

The others had gone back to Ben Southwell, but before I switched off again they were quizzing Charlotte about her sister. Between you and me, Michelle's a bit of a tart – all blonde from a bottle and pierced navel, but she's the only older sister we've got between us, and we're kind of fascinated to have some of her experiences second-hand. Michelle gets away with murder as far as I can see, running Charlotte's parents ragged with her parties and clubbing. Michelle goes out at night when Charlotte comes in. All of which means that their parents are tougher on Charlotte because they can't stand the strain a second time around. Luckily Charlotte's a very different kettle of fish – clubbing's not her scene anyway. Right now Michelle's in Corfu with her friends after their exams, so I hope she doesn't blow that one for Charl as well.

And so the subject turned back to boys – on holiday this time. Charlotte gets to be with the love of her life each year in the Lake District – not that she stands much of a chance, because he's eighteen. Maddy's a complete romantic – she's determined to meet a 'real lovey-dovey Mr Darcy' of her own. Sounds like the older man to me. She'll probably get one on a trip to Barbados with her dad.

It was Maddy's idea that we should all have holiday romances. Fine for her – perhaps not so easy for the rest of us. *'Let's all agree to have holiday romances, and we'll have another sleepover on the last weekend of the holidays and report back.'* She was warming to her subject. *'We'll go round and say where we're going. Age order. I'm nearly fifteen – God, would you believe it – so I go first. OK. I'm going to Barbados with my dad. Two weeks. What about you, Duck?'*

Duck is me. I'd better explain. As if being called Hannah Gross wasn't bad enough, I answer to the ghastly nickname of 'Duck'. Most people just think it's a term of endearment, but in my case it's because I waddle – or used to, when I was still wearing over-large lace-ups (of course my mum had to buy expensive sensible shoes big enough for me to grow into, never the trendy ones I really wanted) in the juniors. And the nickname's stuck, even at my secondary school. It could be worse, I suppose, but sometimes I almost forget I've got a nice ordinary name like Hannah.

I thought about the romance potential of the music course. It's a residential for the good musicians in our area, so it's subsidised, which means that rather than the usual wet boarding-school kids whose parents don't know what to do with them in the holidays, some of the guys are quite normal people. I've played in concerts with quite a few of them and – well, yes, there are one or two I could fancy. In fact, there's even one who looks like John Lennon . . . Still, I don't expect anyone to notice a four-eyed waddler like me. And even if they did, I can't see myself having the confidence to work it into a snogging situation, let alone anything more. Then again, it's high time I did a little experimenting in that direction . . . Not so fast, Hannah old girl, I told myself. Anyway, I might not want to when the time came. No – I wasn't promising anything. The others were looking at me. Oh yes, they wanted to know what I was doing on holiday.

'Me? Oh the usual boring old music course. Ten whole days with a load of musos in sandals,' – which was actually the most likely scenario.

Charlotte went all wide-eyed. 'But I thought you really liked doing your music. And mightn't you meet a wonderful double-bass player or a sexy saxophonist or someone?'

Well, she had a point – the John Lennon one plays the saxophone as well as the flute – but I wasn't going to get my hopes up. 'I might,' I said cautiously, 'but I don't promise to talk about it afterwards.'

'Spoilsport!' said Sophie – but I wasn't going to say anything I might regret, so I kept my mouth shut. Sophie carried on, 'I'm going to yet another campsite in France. With one boring older brother. Mum and Dad read and drink and go to museums and markets. I'm left with dear Danny to mingle with all those other campers. I suppose I might just find myself a Campsite courier on a bicycle . . . You're so lucky, Mads. Barbados, huh? You'll have to have a wonderful exotic time for all of us.'

Some time later, when Charlotte and Maddy were asleep, Sophie and I carried on in whispers. 'I think you're a fraud,' said Sophie. 'You're just as keen as the rest of us. And just as likely to pull. You've got a heaving bosom there, Duck. Don't think we haven't noticed. As for the smouldering eyes behind the librarian specs – ' here she put on an American-movie accent and a deep voice – 'My, but you're beautiful Miss Goldbaum . . . ' Sophie doesn't miss much. And heaving bosom sounds more promising than top-heavy. Obviously it's all a matter of attitude. Where would I be without my mates? It's amazing how a couple of well-chosen phrases can make you feel good about yourself. I snuggled into my sleeping-bag and dreamed of a passionate encounter with John Lennon. In his younger days of course, when he was alive.

Two

Sophie lives round the corner from me. I've known her even longer than the others – since we were toddlers. We pop in and out of each other's houses all the time during the holidays – I like the sense of a caring family and the comfortable muddle in hers and she likes the lack of it in ours. She called round at lunch time. J was out, so I was on my own. Sophie followed me through the hall to our newly done-up kitchen. 'Wow, Hannah. This must have happened since last time I came over. It looks like something out of a magazine.'

'That's because it is. Mum said, "That's a nice kitchen, I'll have that." So, three weeks and ten workmen later, hey presto!' I took her on a tour. 'Walk-in fridge, industrial stainless-steel hob, double oven, microwave, breakfast bar, dishwasher . . . ' Everything's disguised behind identical doors, so you need the running commentary.

'Cool,' said Sophie. 'OK, where's the deep-freeze with the pizza? I'm starving.'

'How about on the end of the phone?'

'But I haven't brought any money for food—'

'No worries. Guilty parents pay all.'

'I'm not complaining,' said Sophie. 'Quattro fro-maggi please.'

I ordered pizzas with extra garlic bread. 'What shall we do this afternoon?'

'We're going shopping,' said Sophie. 'I want a bikini for France and I said we might meet up with Charl at the shops. Why don't we try some on?'

'I'm not sure they make them in 36D. Anyway, my black regulation swimsuit is probably about right for the nasty pool at the school where the course is being held.'

'Oh, go on. You'd look great. Knock 'em dead.'

'Thanks, Sophie.'

'No – I mean you'll look stunning—'

'It's OK,' I laughed. 'I know what you mean. All right. I'll try. So long as they have cubicles in the fitting room and you promise not to laugh!' I looked at my watch. 'Pizzas'll be here in about 20 minutes. I'll go and shave my legs.'

'Wait for me,' said Sophie.

We got on the bus to the shopping centre feeling fat from the pizzas but with wonderfully smooth legs. Somtimes I wonder how I look next to Sophie. Just all wrong compared with her all right, I expect. All tense and anxious compared with her laid-back and hip. Oh well. 'Where are we going to look, Soph?' Sophie knows about clothes and the right places to shop for them. If my wretched mother had her way, I'd be buying everything from John Lewis or Marks and Sparks with a quick turn round C & A for something 'up to the minute'. Sophie wouldn't be seen dead in C & A (really, she just won't even go in) and Marks is strictly for underwear. She'd really like to buy stuff from Kookai and Morgan but Top Shop and Miss Selfridge will do. As far as I can tell, it's more important where you *don't* go . . . but I'm perfectly happy to leave that to Sophie and her highly tuned cool-detectors.

'Top Shop.' Sophie was leading the way. 'First stop.'

Top Shop it was. And there was Charlotte over by the bikinis. Sophie grabbed a handful of hangers. She seemed confident that she'd look fine in almost anything – which is probably true. Charlotte was wavering. I spotted her discarding the horizontal stripes – she's as self-conscious about her bottom half as I am about my top half. As for me, I just wanted something underwired. And I actually found it, in a tasteful greeny colour. I hovered over the black – I always do – but Sophie noticed and reprimanded me, 'Hannah! No!' So I moved towards the more interesting colours.

Not long after, we all emerged from our cubicles. I had to peer at myself because I'd taken my glasses off, but I actually didn't look so bad, especially if I stood up straight. Sophie of course looked gorgeous. But so did Charlotte. Quite a surprise! 'Buy it!' I told her. 'You can seduce Josh in it!'

'And you buy that one, Hannah,' said Sophie to me. 'You look fantastic! As I said earlier, knock 'em dead!' I pretended I hadn't heard precisely what she'd said, and bought it anyway.

Charlotte had to go and finish her packing so she came as far as Boots with us and then left. Sophie wanted nail varnish and I, worse luck, needed to stock up on the really exciting things in life, like sanitary protection. I bought several varieties to be prepared for all eventualities. Sophie looked pityingly at my basket. 'Looks like you're all set for a marvellous holiday Han, hon,' she said. 'Come on, let's go and buy you some gorgeous make-up like Maddy used on you the other night. Just so you can *look* as if you're enjoying yourself even while you're doubled up with period pains.'

'Like, paint a false smile on my face?'

'Something like that.'

Between us we sorted out eyeliner and the brownish eyeshadow. Finding the right lipstick was harder because you can only try it out on your hand. Sophie picked one that I reckoned was darker and vampier than Maddy's, but by then I wanted to pay for my embarrassing basketload and get it all hidden away in a nice carrier bag, so I tossed it in anyway. The queue was full of people buying stuff for going away. I put my basket down and Sophie and I got intrigued by all the different sun preparations the couple in front of us were buying, not to mention the colourful selection of condoms. Terrible how nosy you get in the chemists. At last my things were going through, but by then I was distracted all over again by a loud Scottish voice coming from the large Scottish woman in the queue behind us. She was with a teenage boy who looked totally excruciated and as if he'd rather be anywhere else than in Boots with his mother. 'Donald,' she boomed, 'Do you really shave often enough to need your own shaving cream to take away with you? Couldn't you manage without for a week? I'm sure very few of the other lads your age will be shaving. And do you really need this expensive anti-dandruff shampoo? And Donald, the OXY TEN is a very costly (she pronounced it 'corstly') brand of spot cream.' She picked up the offending article and scrutinised it. Then she tutted, 'You don't have to believe all this advertising nonsense, you know. Now TCP always worked for me . . . '

Sophie was heaving in silent agony next to me. I was sobered by the thought that the boy would no doubt have seen all my ghastly purchases. I glanced back at him after I'd paid. My God! He was tall with longish hair and round glasses and looked remarkably like John L—

'Outta here! Now!' said Sophie and dragged me outside to a bench where we both collapsed. 'Dornald!' she said in her best Scottish accent. 'Dornald, you are a pubescent git with bumfluff, dandruff and zits, and as you're my son I think you should be ashamed of yourself . . . Sad bloke, eh Hannah?'

I hesitated, thinking of the poor guy's embarrassment, not to mention the way he looked, but then I

joined in with her helpless giggles. 'Yeah. Unbeliev-
able.'

Sophie was still gasping on the bus and barely over
it when we got off and bumped, literally, into yet
another embarrassed teenager, the famous Ben
Southwell. 'Hi Sophie!' His voice was rather gruff
(no bumfluff, zits or dandruff though).

'Oh, hi Ben,' said Sophie languidly and started to
walk away.

I wasn't having this. 'Aren't you going to introduce
me?' I asked.

'Ben, meet Hannah,' said Sophie. There was a
silence. 'Hannah, meet Ben,' she added.

I was aware of Ben groping for something to say.
'Maddy gone off somewhere exotic then?' was what
he came up with.

'Oh yes,' I said quickly, terrified that Sophie was
going to remain silent. 'Hasn't she Sophie? She's
gone to the West Indies with her dad, lucky thing.
And Sophie's going to France—'

'You never told me that,' cut in Ben to Sophie. 'I'm
going to France too. Isn't that a coincidence?'

'It's a big place, France,' said Sophie. 'Sorry, Ben.
Hannah and I are in a bit of a hurry . . . '

'Are we?' I started to ask, but she just linked her
arm grimly in mine and walked me away.

'See ya,' said Ben, forlornly I thought, to our
departing backs.

All Sophie's mirth had evaporated. 'Why did you have to tell him I was going to France?' she wailed.

'I'm sorry. I didn't know it was classified information. Anyway, it's a big place, France.' Sophie managed a partial return to normality.

'No. I'm sorry. Sense of humour failure on my part. I'll tell you about Ben Southwell some time . . .'

'I know about Ben Southwell. He kisses like a fish . . .'

'There's more.'

'Well I can tell you one thing. He fancies you like mad. And he's fit. And I'm jealous. And I'll tell you another thing. Donald is coming on my music course. I recognised him, though he was about a foot shorter last year.'

'Hanny, sweetheart . . . ' My mother was using a tone of voice that meant bad news. I'd just packed my bag, folded my music stand and checked that I had a selection of pencils with rubbers on the end – standard music course requirement. Conductors love humiliating kids who don't have their pencils with them. 'Hannah?' Mum's voice came wheedling up the stairs again. 'We need to sort something out darling, could you come down?'

I went down slowly, sliding against the banister. 'What?'

'Don't say "what", Hanny.'

'What do we need to sort out?'

'Your lift to the course tomorrow morning.'

'What is there to sort? You're taking me, aren't you?'

'Well. You see, I hadn't realised you started on a Thursday and unfortunately I now have a meeting . . .'

'But Mum! You promised. Cancel the meeting. Say you've got a prior engagement. You *have* got a prior engagement.'

'I'm afraid it's rather an important meeting.'

'It's important that you take me, Mum! I've got loads to carry. How am I supposed to get there?'

'I was thinking perhaps you could ring one of your friends on the course and ask for a lift?'

'Mum! I don't have any *friends* on a music course. At least, there's no one I know well enough to cadge a lift from!' I was feeling ridiculously upset.

'There is a train, too. You could get a cab from the station. I don't mind giving you the money!'

'I bet you don't!' I snarled. 'You never mind giving me money! It's just a tiny bit of your precious time that you can't give me! You've known about this for ages. Why should your ruddy meeting be more important than your ruddy daughter? Why can't your ruddy daughter come first for a change?'

My dad came home at this point. He always looks dreadful when he comes in from work. 'Now, now, what's all this?' he asked in diplomatic tones as he poured himself a drink. 'No need to fight, surely, not just before you go away darling.'

'Mum won't give me a lift tomorrow. She wants me to go on a train. It'll mean leaving at some unearthly hour—'

'You've lain in bed till lunchtime every day of the holidays so far,' said Mum unnecessarily. 'It won't hurt you to get up—'

'That's not the point!' I shouted. 'You said you'd take me. I want you to take me. All the others arrive with their doting parents. Why can't I?'

'Maybe I can take you,' said Dad. 'I've got a late start tomorrow.'

'That's because you're taking J, Dad, in the opposite direction.'

'You can't let J down,' said Mum. I couldn't believe this.

'But you can let *me* down? Typical!' I stormed out of the room. God I hate that woman sometimes. She upsets me so much. I stomped upstairs and slammed my door. Why can't I have nice parents, like other people? Dad's not so bad, I suppose. Just feeble. I can't imagine him at work, I really can't.

A while later, J knocked on my door. Ever the peacemaker, J. 'Hannah, why don't you let Dad take you and I'll go on a train. I don't mind. It's about time I got around on my own a bit.' Dad was hovering outside. He followed J in and sat on my bed.

'What time do you start Hannah?'

'We have to be there by half-past ten.'

'And you, J?'

'Half-eleven.'

'OK. I'll take you first, Hannah. You'll be there a bit early, I'm afraid. And then I'll dash back and take J.'

Not-so-feeble Dad. 'Thanks Dad. I'd rather be early than have to find my own way there. I just wish Mum would put me before her work sometimes. And before J, sometimes. It's so unfair.'

Dad didn't say anything. There wasn't anything he could say. Then he gave us what was supposed to be a jolly paternal smile. 'Pizzas all round then, for a treat? I think your mother's too tired to cook tonight.' I kicked J to make sure he didn't tell Dad that we'd ordered pizzas for practically every meal so far this holidays. It would be bewildering enough for Dad when he rang them up and found they already knew his address.

*

Sophie rang quite late. 'Have a cool time Hannah. Don't do anything I wouldn't do!'

'That gives me a lot of scope then!'

'By the way. Ben Southwell. It's a bit difficult. He cornered me last week and came out with all this stuff about being in love with me and wanting me to go out with him. And I blew it somewhat. Because I do like him but I just don't fancy him – and told him so. And Hannah, it was awful, because he nearly cried. I didn't know what to do. So then I tried to give him a hug and he shook me off. He said, "Don't do that! I know you don't mean it!" So I said something about not liking to see a friend sad, especially if it was my fault. Anyway, he went quiet for a bit and then just said – "We are friends, aren't we?" So I said, "'Course," and he went away. And today was the first time I'd seen him since. Difficult one, huh?'

'Poor guy,' I said. 'And poor you, too.'

'I'll say. Anyway, have a fabbo time. Think of me in sunny France. And I'll think of you' – and here the Scottish accent came on again – 'and Dornald!'

'Thanks a bunch!' I said into her barrage of giggles.

Three

They always smell, don't they, schools? This was a boarding-school where they'd spent the last few days cleaning up after the term, so actually it smelt chiefly of polish. Writers try to identify the components of school smells, like chalk and disinfectant and socks, but it can't be done. I'll leave it to you to imagine the smell of the school I found myself in, a long way this side of lunch, on a boiling hot Thursday that was about to turn gorgeous. Sophie would never allow herself to be in this situation. Nor would Maddy. And there was I, sitting on a bed in a spotless dormitory for four, swinging my legs like a five-year-old and unable to make up my mind what to do next.

Dad had delivered me and driven off. As the first arrival I was met in the foyer by all three women staff, smiling far too brightly for the early hour, and one goat-bearded man (even I knew him as the Goat, though his real name was Mr Galt), who was always in charge of getting everyone to the right place at the right time. I was duly welcomed and sent to consult the notices on the boards: endless lists that told us which orchestra we were in, what pieces we were playing, where we were sleeping, what we would be doing the rest of the time – meals, organised games, outings – aargh, what was I doing here on a lovely hot day in July! What had happened to my freedom?

The notice-boards told me that I was in 'Daffodil' (ouch!) dormitory on the first floor, sharing with two sixteen-year-olds I knew slightly, Jessa and Gemma (Jessa was first flute), and another girl my own age. Her name was Adela. Alarm bells rang when I read her name but I wasn't sure why. The notice-boards also told me that I was in the first orchestra playing second flute and piccolo. I am good, though I say it myself, so I wasn't surprised. Fourth flute was one Donald Ogilvie. Thank God we were to be separated by the third flute, another Hannah. (There are a lot of us Hannahs.) I scanned the lists for other names I recognised. There were a couple of horn players I was looking forward to seeing again (from afar) and a drummer who everyone fancies. He would liven things up a bit. There were several other girls I get on with, so perhaps I wasn't in for such a terrible ten days after all.

I'd hauled my stuff upstairs. Still no sign of anyone else arriving. The bright chatter of the three women floated up the stairs after me, punctuated from time to time by the gruff voice and the dry laugh of the goaty man. Each bed had a chest of drawers next to it and there were 'dress cupboards' in a small room down the corridor.

I put my clothes away. I put my toothbrush in the toothmug on the chest of drawers. I went and looked out of the window. The grounds of this school were rather beautiful. There was a covered walkway with roses and honeysuckle growing up it, and a huge ancient chestnut tree with a circular bench around the trunk. Beyond the dried-out playing-fields in the distance I could see the swimming-pool, with its Portakabin changing rooms. School buildings and staff houses merged into the trees and hedgerows of the surrounding countryside. Everything shimmered in the heat. Then I heard a couple of cars draw up on the gravel at the front of the school, but that was round the corner where I couldn't see. All of a sudden my solitude seemed precious. I went back to my bed and curled up with a book, so that if anyone came in I could look busy.

Someone swung into the room and hurled a backpack on to the bed next to mine. 'Wattadump' was what she said. 'You Hannah?'

'Yup.'

'Gemma and Jessa are older, aren't they?' she said. I realised that this bright-eyed girl with wiry black curls, shredded jeans and a tight T-shirt that said *I Like the Pope, the Pope Smokes Dope* on it, was Adela Borelli. Half-Italian, brilliant violinist and total wildchild. 'I'm just nipping outside for a cig,' she informed me. 'Don't go away. I'm relying on you to show me the business. Never done a residential before.'

'Just don't get caught smoking,' I said, rather primly.

'Huh! They won't get me!' laughed Adela. 'Considering they *begged* me to come and lead the orchestra, they're hardly likely to kick me out for something as boring as smoking *cigarettes* are they?' She stuffed her packet of 20 into her jeans pocket and disappeared.

Jessa and Gemma arrived together. Jessa is an English rose; Gemma more of a British bulldog, but they're both nice, dead sensible types, with steady boyfriends.

'Hi Hannah,' said Jessa, recognising me. 'I see we've been promoted to First and Second. They should have made you First, really, but then I don't do the piccolo.' Our instruments were all we had in common at this stage.

'Hi,' said Gemma. 'You realise we've got Adela to contend with!'

'She's OK,' said Jessa, testing the springs on her bed.

'You wait until she gets up to her tricks—'

'And what tricks might they be?' Adela came into the room, reeking of cigarette smoke. 'Come on

Hannah,' she said, as if we were already best mates, 'everyone's going in for this meeting and I want to check out Kevin Hazell, you know, the drummer. I want to see how anyone called Kevin can be as sexy as he's supposed to be. Perhaps it's just because he's got his own car.'

A faraway look came into Jessa's eyes. '*He*'s here is he? Kevin! Let me tell you that Kevin Hazell is – a god. He is tall, he is dark, he has these melting brown eyes that just turn you into a little puddle, he—'

Gemma was looking at her strangely, but Adela was tugging at my shirt. 'Come *on*, Hannah,' she said. 'No time to waste.'

The introductory meeting was held in the old school hall. It was one of the original school buildings, more like a church, with pews. I slid in after Gemma and Jessa, and Adela squeezed in next to me. It looked like I was stuck with her. I felt the temperature rise all down the row as the famous Kevin Hazell sat down next to Adela, followed by a number of the older boys, including, to my horror, Donald. (I couldn't even think of his name without hearing it spoken by the Scottish mother from hell.) Adela managed to elbow Kevin in the ribs and get his attention while we were waiting. Jessa was practically fainting with envy, but Adela simply said – 'So you're Mr Skins, are you? I'm Adela, your leader.'

'It's like policemen!' said Kevin, smiling confidentially at the rest of us, 'Leaders get younger every year.'

'Infant prodigy, me,' said Adela, without a hint of embarrassment.

'Ssshhh!' said Gemma. Our introductory meeting was about to begin.

As the Goat told us all about being punctual for rehearsals and quiet after 11pm I glanced around the hall. There were about seventy of us. Half were exceedingly small. They were the junior orchestra, annoying little brats to a kid. The other half were the senior orchestra – us. Most of us were fourteen or over, with a good proportion of sixth-formers. If my row was anything to go by, there were some OK people here. By the time one of the smiley women was talking about what was on offer apart from music I was beginning to think it might even be quite fun – if only to watch Jessa and Adela doing battle over Kevin. He was nice though. When he'd smiled at us I could almost believe he was smiling just at me . . .

Our days were to go something like this: sectionals in the morning and whole orchestra sessions in the afternoon. The afternoon sessions didn't start until about three, so there was a big break in the middle of the day to rest or swim, play tennis, go to the town or whatever. The rehearsals went on until half-five, when everyone rushed to the TV room before supper at half-past six. And then the long summer evenings were our own. Friday nights were disco nights – sarky shrieks and whistles in response to this. It didn't match up to the clubbing habits of the more sophisticated ones.

The juniors trooped out to the other school hall to be briefed about the music they were going to be playing while we stayed behind to hear about ours. This was to be quite a big, showy concert with a Beethoven symphony, Rimsky-Korsakov's Capriccio Espagnol – which has loads of solos for all the different instruments, and the Mendelssohn violin concerto, starring guess who? Adela rolled her eyes at me and wriggled like a little kid. We were also going to put on a chamber concert. We'd form our own groups and choose our own music, including jazz and rock as well as old stuff. Only the really dedicated parents make it to the chamber concert on the last afternoon. Mine never do. They just about manage to arrive in time for the evening concert before whisking me home.

The meeting finally came to an end with, 'You'll be working hard, but we'll try to make this an enjoyable ten days for you. You're all excellent musicians or you wouldn't be here. You all have plenty in common. Get to know each other. (Cheers and jeers.) Have fun. But first have some lunch. The canteen is along the covered way and round the corner. Your afternoon rehearsals are in the gym at three. Sectionals in the music block in the morning.'

We filed out in our rows to the canteen. I was keen to avoid Donald. I'm not sure why. I associated him with feeling horribly embarrassed. From where I sat in the canteen I had a good view of the boys' table. Adela and Jessa were gazing at it – and Kevin – unashamedly, but I just sneaked little looks every now and then. Kevin was unbelievably attractive. Kind of dark and hunky with eyes like deep pools. I couldn't help noticing that Donald's longish, light-brown hair was clean and silky (and dandruff-free!) today. His pointy nose and glinting granny glasses still made him look like John Lennon, but the part of his face that intrigued me most was his mouth and the way the corners went up when he smiled – and that was *just* like John Lennon . . .

'Cool guy, Kevin,' said Adela. 'Jessa was right about his eyes. When he fixes you with his gaze you kind of – wibble.'

'I'm surprised anything makes *you* "wibble", Adela,' said Gemma sharply.

Adela scraped her chair noisily and stood up. 'Anyone else coming for a smoke?' she asked loudly. There was no response so she swaggered off on her own.

'Nice butt,' came a comment from the next table, but it wasn't from Kevin, or from Donald.

'Nice but what?' someone else asked.

'Naughty,' I said, and left the canteen, thinking I might join Adela, at least for a wander round the grounds, if not for a smoke. There was always a chance that some of the attention showered on her by the boys might rub off on me.

The afternoon rehearsal was going fine until I felt a familiar griping sensation in my stomach and realised I was going to have to get to the loo fast. My period had chosen this precise moment to begin. I lasted out to the end of the section and then made a dash for it. Of course I sent my music stand flying, but I couldn't hang around to pick it up. When I came back the entire orchestra was waiting for me. Why is a girl's life so ghastly? I picked my way over to my desk. Someone had righted my music stand. Jessa and the other Hannah were poised ready to play. It was Donald who leant across and pointed out which bar we were starting on. I sensed his sympathy but I couldn't bear to look him in the eye. Of course, he would *know* why I'd had to go out. Ooooh. Horrible! I cringed and tried to concentrate on the music in front of me.

Four

At quarter to eight on Friday morning we were all woken by a nasty buzzing sound. As I surfaced I realised that this was the 'rising bell'. 'Wozatt?!' Adela shouted in alarm. Jessa looked distinctly bleary, but Gemma sat up and looked at her watch.

'Time to get up,' she said, and swung her legs out of bed.

'When'ssectionalsh?' asked Adela.

'Ten o'clock,' I told her.

'Wake me at ten to,' she said, and burrowed back under her pillows.

I had a vague memory of Adela going out in the night. Perhaps that was why she was tired. I decided not to mention it. Jessa wasn't thinking about Adela. She was hugging her knees and looking dreamy. 'When I'm with Kevin I wonder if I should stay with my boyfriend,' she was saying. 'Is it fair, d'you think, to stay with one boy when really you fancy someone else?'

'Doesn't everyone fancy Kevin, though?' I asked hesitantly. *I* fancied him. He even made Adela feel wibbly.

'Well, yes,' said Jessa. 'But he is very nice to me. He

just makes me feel . . . so . . . special when he talks to me.' So the confidential smile hadn't been for my benefit after all.

'Ah well,' she sighed. 'Perhaps I'll get a smoochy dance out of him at the disco tonight . . . '

'Dream on,' said Gemma, returning to the dormitory. 'You're awful, Jessa. You've got a perfectly nice boyfriend of your own. Maybe I should tell him you're more interested in someone called *Kevin*.'

'Oh don't be so boring, Gemma,' said Jessa mildly, and drifted off to have a shower.

'Sectionals' are when each section of the orchestra – strings, brass, woodwind and so on – practise separately. So my section, the woodwind section, consisted of four flute players, three oboists and one cor anglais player, three clarinettists and two bassoonists. Two of the clarinettists, Josie and Helen, were girls I knew slightly from another class at my school. The third, Max, was a boy a bit younger than me who I've played alongside for years. No one had arrived to take the sectional when I got there. Jessa, Hannah and Donald were all in their seats. I had to squeeze past Donald to get to my stand but I was spared looking at him because Josie and Helen were tugging at me.

'Duck! Duck!'

Donald ducked, but I chose not to notice. He

wasn't to know it was my nickname. Yet. 'Duck,' said Josie, 'give us the goss on Adela. She's in your room isn't she? Did you know that she went up to the boys' rooms last night? Apparently she just walked into the room Kevin was in and asked if any of them wanted to come out and wander around with her. They were out for hours. Max says they went for a swim.'

'What did I say?' asked Max, sitting down and adjusting his stand.

'About Adela and the boys last night. Didn't they go for a midnight swim or something?'

'I didn't hear about a swim. I just heard about a hip flask . . .'

'I heard that she was snogging Ke—' Helen was interrupted by the piercing voice of Miss Claggan, the woodwind tutor.

'Quiet, everyone please. We're going to work on the Beethoven this morning, but we're starting with the slow movement – that's page six in your music. Now hands up if you *haven't* brought a pencil with you . . .'

'Here we go,' muttered Jessa.

We had a coffee break at 11.30, and then carried on relentlessly. The worst bit in sectionals is when you have to deal with a particularly tricky bit and everyone has to play those few bars on their own. That way the tutor can find out precisely who is playing the bum notes. The flutes had a difficult ten-bar section. Jessa played it. Most of it was OK. I played it. I fluffed the first few notes and then it went fine. The other Hannah made a complete mess of it. 'Again,' said Miss Claggan. Hannah managed a bit better. 'Once more,' said Miss Claggan. Hannah scraped through. Then it was Donald's turn. I hadn't really heard him play solo. He played it with a very breathy jazzy tone, but it was all in tune and on time. Miss Claggan didn't say anything. Donald started to go red. Then – 'We have a problem here,' said Miss Claggan. Donald looked around desperately.

'Sounded fine to me,' I said to Jessa, as Donald wiped his sweating palms on his jeans.

'Not your playing,' said Miss Claggan, preoccupied. 'No, it's your names, flutes.' Donald looked relieved but we were all puzzled. 'Two Hannahs,' she said. 'What shall I call you, Hannah One and Hannah Two? Hannah with the specs and Hannah without?' Great, I thought, but worse was to come. 'Or your surnames?' (Yeah, call me Gross, why don't you?) 'Does either of you have a nickname I can use perhaps?'

Oh God. 'Hannah Gross is always called Duck!' squeaked Josie.

'Duck?' said Miss Claggan.

'I'd rather not,' I said, but I said it too quietly.

'OK, Duck it is!' said Miss Claggan cheerfully.

And then someone said what was bound to be said sooner or later – 'At least she's not sitting next to Donald!' Total collapse of woodwind section. Donald Duck! Ha ha! At my expense. And Donald's I suppose. He looked over at me but I looked away. It was all too painful. Fancy being 'Duck' here. From now on our names would be horribly, inextricably linked.

In fact the sectional was fine after that. In a funny sort of way the business over the names had broken the ice and made us a group. The only person really suffering was the other Hannah because she was terrible at sightreading and minded about being shown up. But she was a great one for locking herself into a practice room for hours, so she'd sort herself out over the next few days. The piece was even beginning to take shape by the end of the morning. This is when I realise how much I enjoy playing in a orchestra. It's the team thing. You all work away at your little bit and then suddenly you put it all together and it sounds terrific. That part never fails to give me a buzz.

But I wanted more than ever to avoid close encounters with Donald. I stuck with Helen and Josie for lunch, rather than sitting with my room-mates, who were sharing a table with the boys. I caught sight of Adela squashed in between Kevin and Donald, flirting outrageously with both of them. Jessa was looking grumpy and Gemma was being aloof.

'Thanks a bunch for telling the world my nickname,' I said to Josie, as we finished eating.

'Sorry. It just seemed the obvious solution. All your friends call you Duck, don't they?'

'My *friends*, yes. But not the whole world.'

'I really am sorry.' Josie was genuinely apologetic.

'Just don't do it again!' I said, and we all laughed.

Adela scampered over to our table. 'Coming for a walk, Ducks?'

'Not you, as well! Anyway, it's Duck, not Ducks. OK, Adela. I've had enough of this lunch. See you later, you two.'

The bright sun blinded us after the dark of the dining room. High noon in high summer. Mad dogs and Englishmen. The short grass was dry and prickly. The path was a glare of white concrete. Adela was making for an avenue of lime trees which ran along one side of the games pitches. There was a dip between the two rows of tall trunks, so you could sit in the shade with your back against a trunk, well hidden from the passing world. Obviously the perfect place to smoke. Adela lit up. 'Sure you don't want one?'

'No thanks.' But I let out a tremendous exhalation when she did. 'Phew. It's good to be away from everyone.'

'You bet. Everyone's been on at me about last night as if I'd done something really out of order. Such a bunch of goody-goodies. The rumours are cool, actually. Much better than what really happened.'

'Well what did happen? I vaguely remember hearing you go out in the night.'

'What have you heard?'

'Oh, most things. Drink. Sex. Nudity.'

'I told you the rumours were cool! I went over to the boys' block – just for a laugh. Most of them were tucked up in their little beds. Some of them were watching a TV. The younger ones were having a pillow fight, for God's sake! They barely noticed me, but then Kevin came along in these really vile pyjamas to stop them. *He* certainly noticed me! So I said, "You're not really going to bed before eleven o'clock on a hot summer night, are you? Why don't you come outside with me for a bit? We could go skinny dipping." I only said it to freak him out. Anyway, he told the kids to go to bed and then said that he couldn't *possibly* set a bad example by coming with me, but behind their backs he made swimming motions and held up ten fingers. Then he said, all prefect-like, "You'd better get out of here before someone catches you, Adela." I told him that no one had even noticed me so far. It's because I look like a boy, Hannah. Short hair and no bum. Do you know, I walked down the stairs and out of the front door and still no one saw me?'

And that's what she wants, I thought. Attention.

All the time. People to notice her. Look at me! Adela is quite unlike anyone I've ever met in my life before. Not a kid, but certainly not grown-up either. I'm not sure I like her but I can't help feeling envious of her confidence.

'Anyway, I had a swim and then Kevin turned up. He had his jeans on but I could see his pyjama trousers sticking out underneath. And a T-shirt. Gorgeous and hunky he may be, but secretly I think he's a bit of a mummy's boy. He sat on the edge with his feet in the water and said he didn't want a swim. So I pushed him in! He was furious at first – all his clothes wet – but then he just started mucking about, like me. It was cool. Then we came over here and had a bit of a chat while I had a cig. He's OK. Bit of a wuss, but OK . . . '

'OK?' I said. 'OK? He's so fit, Adela. I can't believe you're being so casual. I mean, he followed you out to the pool – just you and just him. I suppose he must fancy you . . . '

'Probably,' said Adela. 'But I suppose I really wanted all of them to come out. It's daft, everyone being in their rooms. It wouldn't happen in Italy. We're all out in the summer evenings, kids, everyone. I thought Donald and the Horns might come out too.'

She looked at me in that direct way of hers. 'What do you think of Donald? Don't you think he looks like John Lennon?'

I was thrown, so I played for time. 'Yes. He does look like John Lennon. I don't know what I think of him.' I thought of Sophie and me in Boots and my dash to the loo and the Donald Duck jokes and the memory of each occasion made me cringe all over again.

'I think he's sexy.'

'Sexy? Donald?' (I thought of the dandruff shampoo and the spot cream.) 'I don't. No. I don't think Donald's sexy—'

Adela's butterfly mind was darting all over the place. 'You ever been to Italy?'

'We stayed in a hotel once, but I don't remember much about it.'

'I go there every summer. It's where I'm going after this is all over. I stay with my Nonna – my Dad's mum. And she lives in this brilliant place with all my dad's other relations. I've got five uncles and loads of cousins. Dad's a bit of a dead loss. He has what we call a drink problem, does my darling papa. Wonderful singer but can't stay upright. That's why Mum has to work so hard. Concerts every night.'

'What does she play?' I didn't want to halt Adela's flow. All this was fascinating.

'Cello. Surely you've heard of her? Celia Barnes? That's her maiden name. Anyway, holidays are a bit of a bummer, or they would be if I couldn't go to Italy.'

'So do you speak Italian with your grandmother?'

'Of course!'

'And do you take your violin?'

'Of course!' she said again, and laughed. 'OK, so they forced me to practise when I was little. No way out when both your parents are musicians. But yes, I still do loads of practice out there because someone always rolls up to listen. And you know me, I love an audience.'

Adela's mind darted back. 'I refuse to be treated like a six-year-old. No one's making me stay in bed if I don't want to be there . . . ' And off again. 'I think Donald's sexy. I think you're lucky sitting almost next to him. He's very tall, isn't he? I like tall blokes. I think he fancies me. I think Kevin does too. And I think I'll probably go for Kevin. Just to annoy Jessa!' Adela leapt to her feet. 'Come on, let's go and see what everyone's doing. There's still an hour before you have to listen to me in whole orchestra rehearsal.'

We spent most of that hour touring the various places people had scattered to. Jessa, Gemma and Co. were sunbathing by the pool. Kevin, Donald et al. were getting sunstroke on the tennis courts. Josie and Helen, Max and some of the younger boys were on the bench under the chestnut tree. Most people were drifting back to the dormitory blocks to get ready for the afternoon rehearsal. Adela abandoned me and went to practise. We were doing the Mendelssohn – her big moment, or rather, moments. It is a difficult and showy solo part, though I don't think anyone doubted that she would manage it.

An hour later, 'manage' wasn't the word I'd have used to describe Adela's performance. Wretched girl had us spellbound. I had that silly lump in the throat and lurking tears you get when something is just completely brilliant. There was little Adela, looking like a sprite or an elf with her short hair, short shorts and a green top, completely into it, ducking and swaying as she played, in a world of her own. We all burst into spontaneous applause when we got to the end. Kevin gave her a drum roll. Jessa leant over to me and said 'Wow. Why do the rest of us bother?'

Adela came and took up her place at first desk again and we carried on the rehearsal. There was plenty of work if we were going to do Adela justice. And even when the rehearsal was over and we were having our dose of pre-supper TV, people were still talking about her. I began to feel I was sharing a room with royalty. The coming evening's entertainment – the disco – hardly got a mention. The boys were all over her at supper, I know, because Adela forced me to sit at their table. Jessa tried to distract them by talking about the disco. 'You are coming, aren't you? You won't all just go to the pub?'

'Now there's a good idea,' said Kevin.

'I don't fancy our chances,' said Donald, who I know is at least two years under drinking age (not that I'd dream of saying anything). 'Staff are all on their guard. I expect *they'll* all come to the disco, Jessa.' And he grinned at her. And it was at that precise moment that something happened to me. That grin. A shake of his hair, his fine silky hair. His eyes dancing behind the glasses. His lanky body leaning towards her. A stab of pure jealousy shot through me. I felt jealous of Jessa because Donald was smiling at her.

Get a grip, Han old girl, I thought. I remembered with renewed pangs all the times he'd tried to be nice to me. How unpleasant he must have found me. Always looking the other way. Always blanking him.

Adela was talking to me. 'You OK over there? You won't catch me going to a totally narcotic-free rave-up, but you'll go, won't you Hannah?'

Oh yes. Dreary innocent little me. Disco queen. Sure. 'I might.'

'Well *we're* going,' said Gemma, linking arms with Jessa and heading for the door, 'and we expect to see you all there.'

'What an incentive,' said Kevin. But I couldn't tell

whether or not he was being ironic. My brain was shot to pieces.

Five

I hate discos.

Adela was nowhere to be seen, but Gemma, Jessa and I spent the next hour getting ready. I had clammy hands (why was I nervous?) and couldn't decide what to wear. I tried on a dress of Jessa's. It looked OK, but then I thought jeans would be better, so I tried on a variety of everybody's tops until I came up with one of Gemma's that suited me. Jessa made me up, so I decided to brave it without my glasses. In the end we tottered over to the new hall, Jessa looking like a tart and me almost completely blind.

The hall was bleak. There were a few older kids, including Max, but mainly there were about fifty brats skidding around to some girl band in the half-darkness. No sign of any of 'our' boys. Jessa (bless 'er) hauled some bloke on to the floor and called to us to join them. Well, we tried dancing, but it was hopeless. I couldn't see much anyway – though I knew it was Max I was dancing with at that point. Later, when he was over at the hi-fi checking for any half-decent CDs, Adela burst in. 'Come on, you guys. We're all going to the pool. This is for the kids. Blimey Jessa,' she added as Kevin and the other boys drew up at the rear, 'you going somewhere special?' I couldn't see Jessa blushing but I felt it. And Adela's next little gem was for me. 'Don't suppose you'll want to swim in your condition, will you Hannah? You could always come and watch.' I couldn't think of anything to say to that, so I just stood by helplessly as the evening crumbled before my (misty) eyes and everyone over the age of twelve left the disco and followed Adela to the pool. Along with Kevin, Donald, the Horns, Max and anyone the tiniest bit worth spending time with. Except Jessa.

Jessa grabbed my arm and hissed, 'Bitch! . . . I hate her!' as she wheeled me away from the hall in the opposite direction. In fact, on that occasion I think Adela was just opening her mouth without thinking first. But poor Jessa. We found ourselves drifting around the gardens. A warm breeze blew through the evening and it would have been quite romantic in different circumstances. We sat down on the grass. 'How dare she show me up in front of Kevin, like that. And you for that matter.'

'I don't really mind what Kevin thinks of me,' I said, realising with a pang that I *did* care what Donald thought.

'Well I mind a lot. And she knows it. Little madam. She thinks that just because she's a genius on the violin she can get away with anything. She flaunts herself in front of the boys all the time. Why doesn't she just wear a sign saying "I am available. Queue here"?'

'I don't reckon she *thinks*,' I said ' – she just acts on impulse.'

But Jessa wasn't having any of it. 'Don't you believe it. She's a scheming little bitch. She knows I fancy the pants off Kevin and so she's determined to get off with him herself. All right, I know I've got a boy-friend and all that, but that's my problem, not hers. I mean, I don't think she even appreciates just how gorgeous he is, that he's nice as well as good-looking. It's all just a game to her.'

Jessa had a point. It wasn't even animal attraction that drew Adela to Kevin (which it certainly was with the rest of us). It was simply that he was the coolest guy around so she was out to prove herself and annoy Jessa by getting him. Rather a waste somehow.

'We have to make sure that the next disco isn't as rubbish as that one,' I said.

'Perhaps we should get them to have it by the pool and cut out the competition,' said Jessa. 'Actually, that's not such a bad idea. There's a big area between the two changing rooms, where we were sunbathing. We could do a barbecue as well. Perhaps it should just be for the older ones – it'll be our last night.' She was really getting her teeth into this idea. I could see her setting up the big romantic scene with Kevin. 'We could get some fairy lights from somewhere . . . ' At least it had taken her mind off Adela for the time being.

The grass was beginning to feel damp so we got up and walked around. We could hear the thud of the music from the disco and the squeals that drifted over from the direction of the swimming pool. Jessa was talking about Kevin but I found that my mind was filling up with images of Donald – or Donnie, as the boys called him. 'Donnie lad' in Kevin's tones sounded a lot better than 'Dornald' as shrilled by his mother. To think that Sophie and I had found him sad! He was so cute. And that smile. If only he'd direct it at me again. I'd like to have him look down at me from that height with a smile specially for me. Really for me, not just for anyone, like Kevin. How was I going to sit so near him all the time with my newly found awareness? It would be torture. Or would it be bliss? And what if he did bother to look at me? Would it be written all over my face? And then I remembered Adela saying that she thought he was sexy. And me saying I didn't think he was sexy. Oh, what if she told him! Donnie, Donnie, I *do* think you're sexy now . . .

'What did you say?' I must have been gnashing my

teeth audibly. And I'd no idea what Jessa had been talking about. It suddenly felt quite late. As if to rub it in, a bell rang from the belltower – time for the younger ones to go to bed.

'What shall we do?' asked Jessa. 'I don't really want to go over to the swimming pool now. I don't know what I want to do, apart from finding Kevin on his own. Come on, Hannah, think of something. We can't possibly just go to *bed*! Not on a beautiful romantic evening like this!'

I thought about it. 'Let's go over to the pool then. There are over thirty senior orchestra kids around the place. I'm not going to let stupid remarks from Adela stop us from doing what we want to do – which for you is being with Kevin and for me is just being with a bunch of us and not being left out.' (I didn't say what I really wanted to do. Actually I wasn't sure what I'd do right then if I was on my own with Donald.) So we ambled over towards the pool. We could hear people splashing about and shouting, but when we opened the high wooden gate we didn't know who we would find there. Faces just look like blobs to me when I haven't got my glasses on, especially in fading light, so I wasn't bothered, but I could sense the tension in Jessa as we went in.

'Adela's not here—' she hissed.

'Probably in the boys' changing rooms then,' I said tactlessly.

'Hi you two!'

'Who was that?' I asked.

'Max and the two Horns,' said Jessa, still distracted. 'I can't see Kevin either. Or Gemma. Or Donald.'

'I expect Adela's dragged them off for a smoke or something,' I said, not liking to think about it.

'Guess what!' said Max, near us now. 'Big scandal! Adela was swimming topless when the Goat came along. Not that *we* minded of course. She said she was only doing what they do on every beach on the continent, but he wasn't having any of it. He told Gemma to get her a towel and ordered Adela to get out straight away and get dressed and go over to the office. She's in for a rocket.'

'So where are the others?' Jessa asked.

'Well. Gemma went with Adela to the office. A bunch of blokes went off somewhere else. My guess is that they went somewhere in Kevin's car.'

'Right gang of delinquents we are!' I was a bit shocked by Adela's exhibitionism, though not surprised. She was perfectly right about Mediterranean beaches. I mean, my *mother* goes topless there, though I wish she wouldn't.

'No,' said Jessa through gritted teeth. 'Just normal teenagers. Who happen to play musical instruments. The only thing that's abnormal is that we have parents who think it's OK to send us to prison camp in our school holidays.'

'It's not that bad!' said Max. 'We were having a brilliant time until the Goat came along.'

'Max,' said Jessa grandly. 'You are fourteen. I am nearly seventeen. I'm old enough to have left home and I don't like people who aren't even my parents telling me what to do.' This amused me because Jessa is hardly a rebel, but I knew she was sore at that moment. Her darling Kevin with a topless Adela. Hang on! My darling Donald with a topless Adela too, and all the other darlings. Actually I could only think of it as funny. If Adela wanted to take her clothes off it was up to her. I can't say I felt threatened. And it had obviously made Max's day.

'Lemmego!' Gemma was struggling to get something from Adela's hands as we walked back in.

Definitely a situation that needed defusing. 'Hi Adela! You've made a lot of young men very happy tonight!'

Adela finally shook herself free. 'I can't see what the fuss is all about. Fascists. They make me furious!' She glared at Gemma. 'And you, you're as bad as the rest of them! So I want to have a fag. I'm upset. OK? And you get it into your head that I'm going to set fire to things.' She flicked her lighter on under Gemma's nose. 'Angry, yes. Stupid, no. Not like everyone else around here.' She went to the door.

Jessa stepped forward. 'Adela – don't you think – if everyone's cross already—'

'Oh give me a break!' screamed Adela and pushed past her on her way out.

'Thank God you're back,' said Gemma. 'She's completely out of control. Honestly, when the three teachers told her off she went berserk. Two of them frogmarched her back here. They said her behaviour was disgusting and immoral and that they would tell her parents. So she just shouted, "Fine! Do that. My Dad's an alcoholic. My Mum's a professional workaholic. Oh yes, they'll be so upset to discover that their daughter removed her bikini top won't they – like they *really* give a cuss. Well, believe me, they don't!"'

'Adela's just on a different planet from the rest of us,' I said.

'No she isn't,' Jessa said. 'She's a spoilt little brat and a complete exhibitionist. I don't think we should start feeling sorry for her.'

'I don't understand her at all,' said Gemma.

It occurred to me that maybe I was the only one who had any time for Adela. 'I think I'd better go and get her. I know where she goes.'

'She can stay out all night for all I care,' said Gemma.

'As long as she doesn't decide to include Kevin in her plans,' said Jessa, suddenly alarmed.

I managed to slip outside again. I don't know quite

how Adela does it so easily – I had to play hide-and-seek with the teachers and the Goat quite a bit before I crept out of one of the back doors. I wasn't sure how we were going to get in again. I found Adela in the lime avenue as I knew I would. She was alone. 'I came out to keep you company,' I said and sat next to her.

She didn't say anything. She finished her cigarette and stood up. 'We'll go back past the music block', she said. 'The jasmine smells fantastic at night.' Like a lamb she came back with me, sliding in the back door, past the voices coming from the staff sitting room and up the stairs in the subdued light to our room.

She stripped off, got into bed and whispered 'G'night.' So ended the most important day of my life to date, the day I fell in love with Donnie.

Six

The first Saturday on a ten-day course is just like a weekday. (The following Wednesday is an outing and then the second Saturday is the concert before we all go home.) But I woke up feeling completely hyper – like I do on a weekend in schooltime – and wondered why for a while before I remembered. Donnie. Don. Donald. 'Dornald' even. Oh God! I didn't know if I wanted to see him or not. I couldn't decide what to wear. I wished I didn't have to wear my glasses. I wanted it to be a hot day so we could sit outside but then I thought I'd prefer a wet day so we'd be confined indoors. Maybe I'd just stay in bed and daydream for a bit. Adela was dead to the world, but Gemma, in her usual efficient way, was ready for breakfast, and so was Jessa. They looked over to where I was sitting in my nightie with three tops laid out on the bed. 'The black one,' said Jessa. 'Come on, I'm starving.'

'She means that she wants to get over to the dining room to see Kevin,' said Gemma, 'and check that he hasn't been corrupted. But we'll wait for you if you hurry up.' Did I want to have a shower and wash my hair or did I want to see Donald?

'You go. I'll skip breakfast. I want to wash my hair. Bring me back an apple or something.' So I had a shower and washed my hair. I blow-dried it so it hung straight and shiny. Black top. Jeans. Trainers. Glasses. Damn. I wished I didn't have to wear them. If Mum wanted to buy me off this holidays she could get me some contact lenses . . . Squirt of body spray.

'Oi! Hannah! You smell!' Adela was waking up. 'It smells OK actually. Can I borrow some?'

'I suppose so. Hadn't you better get up, Adela?'

'I'll get up when I want to, thank you very much. I'm not letting those cows get to me, you know.'

'Well, sectionals start in half an hour. See you at lunch time?' I could hear Gemma and Jessa coming back from breakfast and I really didn't want to be there when they saw how late Adela was. It was a gorgeous day outside. I gathered up my flute and went out to intercept them. 'Did you bring me back some food?'

'Oh sorry,' said Jessa. 'We forgot. If you run you might still get some. They were only just starting to clear away when we left.' Again I dithered. Did I want food, or did I want to get to the sectional long before Donald so that I didn't have to squeeze past him? I set off towards the dining room, saw the boys leaving it and changed my mind. I headed towards the music block. I was hungry. Well, sort of hungry. I had butterflies in my stomach and my hands were clammy again. I wished I wasn't on my own. I felt self-conscious. What if I bumped into the boys? I thought of Sophie. She wouldn't be fazed like this. She thought Donald was a pubescent git. I looked around guiltily as if someone could read my thoughts. I don't think you're a pubescent git, Donnie. *I* think you're cute.

Needless to say I arrived ten whole minutes earlier than anyone else for the sectional. Max was the next to turn up – with Donald. 'Bit early for sex aren't you

Hannah?' said Max, and grinned over at Donald before they both cracked up. Helen and Josie came along next. There was definitely an air of hysteria.

'Toothsome twosome,' remarked Max, and they cracked up again.

'OK, OK, what's the joke?' said Jessa from the door. 'Are you talking about Adela? Everyone else is.'

Max strutted around pretending to be Adela unclasping her bikini top and tossing it to the crowd. He mimicked: 'Don't gawp, Max. Never seen a girl naked before? I just prefer an all-over tan. You'll get used to it.'

Helen took over. She minced around with one hand on her hip. 'Anyone would think I was doing something *wild*. Where have you been all your sad little lives?'

Then Donald became the Goat arriving on the scene. He stepped back and put his hand over his eyes. 'Good gracious girl! COVER YOURSELF UP!' and the entire section who had now gathered fell about laughing. Jessa caught my eye and silently commiserated. At least I wasn't the only one who'd missed the drama. I couldn't help feeling a bit sorry for Adela being the butt of everyone's jokes, but Miss Claggan was there and organising us before sympathy got the better of me.

People became businesslike as they sorted out their stands and their music. I dared myself to glance sideways at Donald once or twice when I knew he was turning pages or looking at Miss Claggan. The day was becoming hot and airless. I felt aware of my whole body: the way I was sitting, my feet, my hands, my glasses. I realised I was sensing Donald rather than seeing him – his concentration, his nervous smile when he played a wrong note, his outstretched legs when he wasn't playing and the way he tucked one foot under his chair when it was his turn.

What with one thing and another, I was pretty tense. And then – my guts started to speak. During the twenty bars rest my empty tummy started to protest loudly – and musically. Jessa and the other Hannah were the first to titter, and then, as the rumbles became more pronounced, everyone else in the section. Donald and Miss Claggan were the last to surrender to helpless giggles. 'Now, really!' scolded Miss Claggan.

'Those were the most musical notes I've heard all morning!' said Max.

'Donald Duck lives!' said Helen.

'Lunchtime, I think,' said Miss Claggan firmly. 'And Duck – eat breakfast in future!'

Why is my life one big embarrassment? Now everyone was talking to me in Donald Duck voices. Everyone, that is, except Donald. He'd disappeared. He didn't turn up for lunch either. 'Where's Donald, Duck?' Why was everyone asking *me*?

'How should I know?' I said to Gemma.

'Well, you sit with him don't you?'

'And it's funnier to ask you,' said one of the Horns.

'I know where he is.' It was Adela speaking. (How did *she* know?) 'I saw him being kidnapped by the Loch Ness monster – a monstrous Scottish female – straight after your sectional.'

'That's his mother,' I said.

'Oooh, so you *are* very familiar with the life of Donald, Duck!' said Jessa.

'Well – I—'

'Don't protest too much . . . ' said the other Horn.

Adela was impatient to finish her bulletin. 'When I asked him where he was going he said it was his grandparents' golden wedding party and his mother wouldn't let him miss it. He's coming back tonight though. So cheer up, Hannah.'

'What? Me?' What was Adela up to now?

'Yeah. You should have seen your face just then.'

'Oh shut up, Adela,' said Jessa protectively. 'Come on, Hannah. Let's go and sunbathe before the weather breaks.'

'I thought I heard thunder during the sectional,' said Max with a wicked grin.

Did I dare to ask Jessa what was going on? 'Jessa, why do I get the feeling everyone's always taking the mickey out of me?'

'They don't.'

'Well, it feels like it. All this – ' I hesitated, not wanting to give anything away – 'Donald Duck business. And what was Adela on about?'

'Oh, ignore her. She just wants to make people think that she knows more than they do. And . . . well . . . I suppose it's because you do look rather anxious all the time. But it's a cute sort of anxious. And the boys probably fancy you and try to cover it up with teasing.'

'ME!' I couldn't have been more surprised. Maddy, Sophie, yes. Charlotte, maybe. But *me*? There must definitely be signals out there that I was not reading.

'Yes. Why not?'

'Glasses? Bad hair? Top heavy—'

'Exactly. Where've you been, Hannah? You know what blokes go for!'

'Yes. Leggy blondes. Without glasses.'

'Nobody minds glasses these days. It's like train tracks. You won't have them forever. And you're cool. You know about things and you don't blather like most girls.'

I was struck dumb with amazement. With my old friends I was just the Duck. And with the girls at school I was just one of the swotty ones. I wasn't sure I could cope with being noticed.

'So what was that about Donald?'

'Adela thinks he fancies you. Didn't she say? And

she can't stand the fact that someone might fancy anyone other than her, so she's going to make it difficult for you.'

'Oh, Adela's not that spiteful, you know.'

'She is, Hannah. Watch it.'

It was pain and pleasure together to have Donald absent. I didn't have to worry about shooting off to the loo, my glasses steaming up, bumping into him, or anything like that. On the other hand, I missed him. I would glance over to his desk and feel disappointment at his empty chair. Life was dull without the possibility of one of his smiles in my direction. And now Jessa had planted the idea in my brain that *he* fancied *me* . . . Oh well. I was so flustered that I would have blown it anyway.

The thunder came towards the end of the afternoon rehearsal. It was loud and close and made people scream, but it was also a huge relief as giant raindrops hit the windows of the hall. There was to be an early evening concert for the public given by the tutors on the course, followed by a barbecue and silly outdoor games for us. The rain would put paid to our games, though I don't think many of the older ones minded. Saturday night telly was OK entertainment for most of us.

We had to sort out the old hall for the concert. I don't mind humping chairs around and I felt relaxed for almost the first time. No Donald to worry about. The fact that people quite liked me. Having a laugh with Max and Jessa and Gemma and the Horns. No silly games, just a few hours in a darkened common room watching *Blind Date* and other undemanding programmes. So I didn't blush or flinch when Kevin came over to where Jessa and I were setting up music stands (though Jessa did). 'You're sorted for chamber music, aren't you Jess?'

'Yes,' said Jessa comfortably. 'I'm in the wind quintet,' she added, not without pride. The wind quintet was a prestigious group consisting of first flute, first oboe, first clarinet, first horn and bassoon.

'What about you?' Kevin turned his melting gaze on me. I melted. It was a Pavlovian response.

'Me? Oh, I expect I'll just wind up with one bunch of dregs or another. It's all us non-principals expect. Piccolo, triangle and double-bass trio or something.'

Kevin smiled. I wibbled. Another reflex action. And the smile was just for me – sorry Jessa. 'You wouldn't like to join our jazz group, would you?'

I saw Jessa's jaw become completely unhinged. so did mine. 'But what would I play?'

'Well, we really need a saxophonist, but a flute will do. Donald has to be on keyboard, I'm on drums and Sam's on double bass. I do some of the vocals too. You know, the dark brown voice.'

To match his eyes, I thought, not that I was really

capable of rational thought at that moment. Or rational speech. This was just so cool. My favourite music, with, it has to be said, my favourite guys. And they actually *wanted* little me! My glasses were steaming up. I could see Jessa trying desperately to think of a way of weasling out of her wind quintet and offering herself, but she didn't really like jazz, or any sort of busking.

Sound came out of my lips. 'Fine,' I said, sounding a thousand per cent cooler than I felt.

'Excellent!' said Kevin and drifted off, leaving me and Jessa completely poleaxed.

'I won't pretend I'm not jealous,' said Jessa when he was out of earshot and we'd sat down on a couple of stacks of chairs. 'Fancy all that close contact with Kevin. *And* you're one of the younger ones. There, what did I tell you? I said they all fancied you.'

'Jessa! There is no way that Kevin fancies me. If he's any sense, he fancies you. So rest assured on that score. You two are out of my league.' I was about to say that anyway, I wasn't interested in Kevin, I was interested in Donald. But good sense prevailed.

'Adela's nose will be seriously out of joint, too. Still, there isn't really any call for a violin in a jazz band, is there?'

'She's in the string quartet. I know, because she mentioned it yesterday. I'm so chuffed, Jessa! Things are looking up at last!' And they were. I hadn't thought about Donald for a whole minute.

The 'barbecue' had to be sausages and baked beans in the common room. It suited me. It felt very cosy with everyone huddled round the TV and the rain pouring down outside. Admit it Hannah! I was enjoying myself. A lot. Embarrassment and curse notwithstanding. Two hours of telly was enough for some people and there was a move afoot to have a table tennis tournament. Some people obviously still wanted their silly games. Kevin was one of them. In fact, Kevin turned out to be an organiser, and before we knew it we were all involved in round the table tennis – even flat-footed me. And we'd been tearing round the table for a while before I noticed that Donald was playing too.

'Hi Hannah. Has Kevin asked you yet?'

Don't faint Hannah. And don't presume. 'About what?' I asked coolly.

'Will you be in our band?' Great. I'd wanted to hear it from him too. 'I can't play flute or sax because I do the keyboard. Have you ever played sax? I could teach you if you wanted. It's the same fingering as the flute.' He looked closely at my mouth. 'And you've got the right sort of mouth.' Who was babbling now?

'I told Kevin I'd do it.' How did I manage to sound so calm?

'Oh, great. That's brilliant.'

'HANNAH!' shouted Max. 'It's your turn. Stop gassing!'

'Sorry!' I said, and smiled at Donnie. He smiled back and the ball shot past my left shoulder.

As it was Saturday the staff didn't shove us off to bed until well after eleven. Too early for Adela, but I was knackered. The boys were in a huddle as we went off. It didn't occur to me to be suspicious, though I should have been – there was a lot of sniggering going on.

Adela caught up with me. 'I didn't see you this evening,' I said to her, already slightly nervous about her reaction to me being in the jazz band.

'I went to the concert,' she said. 'And then I practised. I think playing table tennis is a bit juvenile.'

'Kevin doesn't.' I was still smarting from her comments at lunch-time.

'That's only because I wasn't around,' she said smugly.

I started to say that it was nothing of the sort and then held back. I wasn't interested in Kevin anyway, and it seemed that she didn't know about the band. I had the feeling that Adela was like an unreliable kitten. Stroke her in the wrong place and she'd scratch.

*

I fell into a deep and happy sleep which turned into an amazingly vivid dream about Donald telling me I had the right sort of mouth and kissing me. I could feel his hair. I could hear his laugh. Wait a minute. I *could* hear him laughing! And Max, and two other boys. I opened my eyes in the half dark as I heard drawers being opened and shut and the sound of things being shoved into a plastic sack.

'What the hell's going on?' Gemma was sitting up, but the culprits had legged it.

'Oi!' Adela was half out of bed.

'I don't believe it!' said Jessa outraged. 'We're the victims of a knicker raid!'

'Ha!' Adela loved it. 'Brilliant! At last! A bit of life round here! Who was it? Where have they gone? What did they take?' And she rummaged, thrilled to bits, through her drawers.

'They've taken all my underwear,' said Jessa, not knowing whether to laugh or be cross.

'Mine too,' I said. I'd been through my drawers, but so had the villains. They'd taken everything except the sanitary towels.

Total joy in the evening gave way to total mortification.

I curled up, miserable. Would the embarrassment never end? 'Night all,' I said, wondering how on earth I was going to face anyone in the morning.

Seven

'It wasn't me who told, honest.' I was angry with them, but I don't grass. Kevin, Don and Sam looked at me, unsure. Predictably it had been Gemma who'd reported the crime in the morning, but it hadn't brought the underwear back. Between them the boys had managed to empty the top drawers of every single one of the senior girls before disappearing into the night. Fortunately we all had our swimming gear to wear instead, but there'd been an uproar. I had a sneaky admiration for the feat they'd pulled off, but I needed a change of knickers. And I didn't like the fact that they'd gone into places that were essentially female and private. Perhaps I wouldn't have been so cross if I hadn't had the curse. But that was part of the point. Girls need their privacy and boys should respect that.

All the boys had all been called into the hall for a talking to – nobody knew precisely who was responsible – and warned that when the culprits were discovered their parents would be told. The usual threat.

'Nothing to do with us,' said Kevin, Sam and Donald, all innocence.

I looked at Donald. 'Oh yes it was,' I said. 'I *heard* you laughing.'

'Such naughty boys,' said Kevin, smirking.

'You'd better tell us where they are – the knickers,' I said. I wasn't feeling shy right then, and I sensed that they were abashed, slightly.

'Ooh,' said Donald. 'It was *knickers* they took, was it now?' Underneath the bravado he was smiling up at me anxiously from behind his glasses.

'I *heard*,' said Sam, 'that they'd stashed them in the freezer.'

'Yes, that's what I *heard*, too,' said Donald.

'Never mind the knickers,' said Kevin. 'Let's get started.'

'I mind the knickers!' I said. 'Just because you smelly lot wear one pair all week doesn't mean to say that we do.'

'Well—' Kevin was quite embarrassed.

'They'd better come back very soon, or the girls are all going on strike.' I'd just made this up. 'And this quartet, for one, will be a trio.'

'OK, OK,' said Kevin. 'We wouldn't want that, lads, would we? See to it that the knickers are returned forthwith!'

'Aye aye, cap'n,' said Don and Sam together, still leering, mind you.

Donald was actually the natural leader of this group. Even Kevin accepted that when Don sat down at the keyboard he was king. I hadn't known he played anything other than a breathy flute and the saxophone. He noodled around for a while and then said, 'Why don't we just start in with something we all know. You all right about jamming, Hannah?'

I nodded. I was.

'What shall we do then?'

Sam started plunking on his bass. '*Yesterday*,' he said. Everyone knows that.

Phew.

So Donald started us off. I just let myself go and tootled in whenever I felt it was right.

The song drew to a close. 'Wow!' said Kevin. 'Hannah, what a star! You're a natural! Did you know that?'

'I like playing without music,' I said. 'I love jazz.'

'You can tell,' said Donald. And he looked triumphantly over at Kevin. 'See? Told you she was the one to ask!'

'After Jessa,' I added.

Kevin coughed. 'Well, I knew Jessa was fixed up really,' he said.

'I didn't want Jessa!' Donald said. 'Thank God she was fixed up! I said to ask Duck. You're impossible Kevin!'

I smiled to myself. Jessa would be over the moon to know that Kevin had invited her against his instructions. It was a wet Sunday afternoon. We'd been allowed a lie-in in the morning – it was that or church. Adela, rather surprisingly, had been to Mass, which meant she wasn't back in time for lunch. I realised how much more peaceful life was without her. Now we were working on our chamber group stuff, and here I was in a large practice room with three guys, and I was getting to know them fast. My righteous anger over the knicker raid gave me an advantage because it meant they were just the tiniest bit deferential. It also overrode my shyness. But more important than anything, they rated me as a jazz player! For the past few days I'd simply admired Kevin from afar. Now I could tell that, as Jessa kept saying, he was a really nice bloke – and an excellent drummer. I liked the way he played, totally relaxed and cool, lots of sexy shoulder movement. When we were playing without music I had every reason to watch him, to try and anticipate what he was going to do with the beat. I enjoyed watching the muscles in his back, and the suntanned gap between his T-shirt and his jeans.

Of course I had even more reason to watch Donald closely, since he led us from the keyboard most of the time. Now here was a difference too. As a fluteplayer he was slightly stiff fingered and uncomfortable looking, especially jammed up with the rest of us in the woodwind section. But on keyboards he was all over the place, head down, hair shaking; or head tilted back, beatific smile on his face; or standing as he played and making eye contact with the rest of us. Wow! Respect! Not only was I in love with the guy but I thought he was brilliant. I felt humbled, so grateful that he'd chosen me. How could I ever have thought he was laughable?

Sam was the quiet one. He just grooved away on his double bass. Like me he took his cues from Don and Kevin. He's tall with heavy dark eyebrows and a serious face which breaks out into a rare cheeky smile.

I found out a lot about myself in that session too. Ever since I was a little kid I could copy tunes I heard and get them right. I thought everyone could, but I still have memories of people exclaiming when I sang some song note for note. I've never had any trouble reading music, but I've always been happiest busking, just like when I was little and playing the notes in my head. So here I was doing this for real. And still impressing people. But these people were not my parents' friends. I wasn't compelled to be an extension of my mother's ego. I was with cool guys. Was I happy? Was I ever! I didn't want the session to end.

At teatime we gave Sam our orders for drinks and chocolate and he went off to fetch them while the three of us sat around watching the rain. Kevin went off to the loo and I was left with Don. I suspect he felt as shy as I did. He stood up and stretched. 'Phew, it's a bit rank in here. Do you think we can open the french windows?' He loped over and managed to wrench them open. A rush of sweet-smelling air came into the room.

The temptation was too great. I stepped outside and stood in the teeming rain for a few seconds. Bliss! When I came back in my hair was wet and my glasses were streaming. I took them off and flicked my hair out of my face, scattering raindrops on to Don. I looked up at him. 'Sorry about that! It's beautiful out there. You've never smelt anything so gorgeous!' And I was rewarded by the briefest of smiles – yes, down at me and me alone – before Kevin returned, closely followed by Sam and the drinks.

I felt more at ease with the others there. We sat on the floor and shared out the picnic. 'OK guys. So where is the underwear?' I asked.

'You could try looking in the place I *heard* they'd been stashed,' said Sam.

'I could,' I said. 'But I'm in the middle of a chamber group rehearsal, aren't I?'

'They'll be returned,' said Kevin, as if he knew.

'They will indeed,' said Don solemnly. And then they all laughed at their own private joke.

Boys! I don't know.

We stood up and brushed the crumbs off ourselves. 'We can do another hour or so if we're up to it,' said

Kevin. 'Perhaps the rain will have stopped by this evening and we can have a swim.'

By the end of the wet afternoon we had worked out four things to play: *Yesterday*, *The Entertainer* (possibly), *In the Mood* and *Take Five*. All tired old favourites, I know, but not when *we* played them! Under Don's direction we worked really well. The only problem was with *Take Five*. 'It's no good,' said Don. 'The flute's all wrong in this.'

I gulped before he added – 'Not your playing – that's brilliant, especially the improvising. It's just that the sound's wrong. It really needs a sax. Can you play the piano, Hannah?'

'Not well enough for this,' I said.

Don thought for a bit and then said, 'How about I teach you the sax then, like I said before? It wouldn't be difficult for someone like you.'

I tried to hide my excitement at the thought of being taught the sax by Don. 'OK. I like trying new things.'

Kevin interrupted. 'Look, I've got to go. I promised Adela I'd listen in on her masterclass.'

I felt buoyed up and brave enough to say, 'Ooh, Adela's masterclass, eh?' in a suggestive way, but I soon shut up when Donald also said that he'd promised to go.

'Oh no you don't, Donnie lad,' said Kevin. Could it

be that he wanted to keep Adela for himself? 'You have knickers to rescue. Don't pretend it wasn't you. We all know it was, amongst others. And I know a certain young lady who won't be happy until her knickers are restored, and we wouldn't want that.'

Donald flashed a glance at me. I looked down demurely, fighting a jubilant heart.

'OK, Duck. Can't have our star player unhappy, can we?'

The cold store was behind the kitchens at the back of the main building. No one was about in the pouring rain. The kitchen staff were still at home recovering from Sunday lunch. Donald and I had to run from tree to tree to get there without being soaked. We moved more furtively as we got closer, and finally made a dash for the cold store door. The padlock hinge was open. I lifted it and pulled open the door. The chill struck us at once and brought goose bumps to our wet skin.

'All right,' I said, surveying the range of chest freezers I could make out in the crack of light from the door. 'Which one?'

'Well,' said Don, 'It wasn't actually me who hid them you understand.'

'Why in a freezer for God's sake?'

'Why not?' Donald was peering into a freezer full of frozen chips. His face was eerily lit up by the blue light inside. 'He said he put them in an empty one. Nothing unhygienic, naturally.'

'Naturally.' I lifted the lid on a freezer full of chicken and fish. 'They're bound to be in the last one we open aren't they?'

'Got them!' yelled Don triumphantly, and held up a frozen bin liner, presumably full of frozen underwear. But then he suddenly ducked behind the freezer and frantically motioned to me to do the same. Someone was approaching. Two people were coming in.

It was two of the kitchen staff with a metal barrow. They switched on the light, a single bulb. 'We'll need three tubs of frozen minestrone from the third freezer on the right,' one of them said. 'Then come and help me load up with baking potatoes from this bunker.' The bunker was by the door. Donald and I held our breath.

They seemed to take forever. We heard all 70 potatoes bonging into the barrow. Donald was clutching the bin liner to him, trying not to let it rustle, though I could see that its icy coldness was just about killing him, until a large wet patch started to develop on his T-shirt as the contents began melting. At last the cooks had everything they wanted. But then disaster struck.

'Turn out the light can you? I'm going to lock up for the night.'

Aaagh! Did I really want to be locked in a dark cold store for the night – even with Donald?

We heard the padlock snapping shut and their footsteps getting softer as they went into the kitchen. 'Oh dear,' came Donald's voice through the darkness. 'What now?'

Eight

At first we just giggled. The whole situation was so ridiculous.

'It could be a long wait,' said Don gravely.

'I know.' I echoed his tone. But that just made us both laugh again.

Don kept on his serious voice. 'They're not going to like it!' he said. 'Not one little bit . . . Oh well!' He put the bag of knickers down. 'I'm rather cold and wet. But I expect I'll warm up. How about you?' Cue, I thought, for something huggy. But no. Anyway, I'd have been too embarrassed just then. 'We could do some jumping-around type exercises,' he suggested.

'No thanks,' I said. It wasn't what I had in mind. 'You can. It'll pass the time.'

He stood up. 'Do you mind if I take off my wet things?'

'I—'

'My T-shirt,' he added, and pulled it off.

My eyes were only just accustomed to the tiny amount of light that came under the door. I didn't want to look. But then he started leaping around, doing what I considered to be bust exercises.

'Canadian army stuff,' he panted. 'They make us do it at school.' And he did some knee bends. I was mesmerised. I've never been that close to a bloke being so physical. His torso gleamed in the faint light. It was a nice, well-built torso. At last he came to rest. 'Phew! Sorry about that. I was getting really chilled. And I lose my inhibitions in the dark!'

Promising, I thought. What next? He pulled his damp T-shirt on again and paced about the cold store. 'I wonder if there's anywhere warm in here?'

'We probably ought to be by the door,' I said. 'Then we can shout if we hear anyone outside. And it might be a bit warmer too, if the sun comes out. If!'

'Fat chance,' said Don. 'You're right though, let's set up camp here,' and he sat down against the wall by the door. He patted the ground beside him and I sat down obediently. There was just enough room for the two of us between the potato bunker and the door but very little to spare. I managed to keep an inch between us, on tenterhooks in case we should

73

accidentally make contact. I wanted to squash up against him, really I did, but then the shy part of me took over and held me rigidly at a distance. God, I hoped someone would let us out soon. The fact that this was a situation made in heaven didn't help. I couldn't cope.

'Sorry – what?' I'd been so wrapped up in my own paranoia that I hadn't heard what Don was saying.

'Oh, nothing really. I was just making conversation.' (Oh dear, was it that difficult?) 'I just asked if you had any brothers or sisters. Not important.'

'I've got one older brother,' I said, 'called Jeremy. Unfortunately.'

'What, that you've got him or that he's called Jeremy?'

'Oh he's not bad, as nerds go. No, I meant that he's called Jeremy. I call him J, which sounds better somehow.'

'Huh.' There was a short silence. 'I'm not in a position to laugh at other people's names. I mean – Donald! It's not so bad if it's said in a Scottish accent, but I'm used to people falling about when I tell them. Funny, isn't it? John's OK, Dan's OK, but Don just isn't quite. It sounds like a sixties pop star.'

I really didn't want to talk about names. Or how ours were linked. 'What about you? Your family, I mean?' I couldn't imagine there being any more where he came from. Especially after seeing his scary mother. But I was wrong.

'I've got two older sisters. Quite a bit older. I was what you might call an afterthought. Or a mistake, more like. When I was little, my friends thought Ma was my grandmother and that Dad was my grandfather.'

'My parents are normal-parent age,' I said. 'But I don't see much of them. I don't think they could be any more useless than they are.'

'Ooh, *bitter*!' said Donald. 'Mine are OK. Mum's bark is worse than her bite. And Dad can be quite a cool dude when she lets him. Really into jazz, you see. But can't play a note – and can't get over the fact that I can! So he's always been a bit indulgent towards his Donnie-lad. Apparently he was resigned to never having someone to wear a kilt with him and then I came along . . .'

'You don't really wear a kilt do you?'

'If you were christened Donald Angus Bruce Ogilvie you'd get to wear a kilt, too! I wore one yesterday if you must know.'

'You must show me some time . . . What about your sisters then? How old are they?'

'Ancient. Twenty-three and twenty-five. I'm a bit like an only child really. It's quite good having big sisters, though, because they make a fuss of their baby brother. I really missed them when they left home and I only had Ma and Dad for company. That's when boarding-school was a good thing. Not any more, though. I'm going to sixth-form college next term.'

'I don't think I could ever call my parents "company". They're desperate for us to achieve great things, but all without their help. Sometimes I just feel mine would prefer a photo of me and a sheet of brilliant exam results. They're not interested in the flesh and blood, and certainly not the heart and soul.'

'Bet that's not true,' said Donald, shifting round slightly so that he was facing me.

I was taken aback. My grotty parents are a fact of life. Who was this boy to say that things should be otherwise? 'So I'm a liar?'

'Not at all. But you know, at school, at night, we quite often talk about our families. Especially with the younger ones, when they're homesick. And so many kids think their parents don't like them. And then they turn up on parents' day and you can see that they're like all the other parents – thrilled to see their little darlings. I just think some adults aren't very good with children. They love them, and everything, but they just don't know how to behave. No one's ever taught them and it doesn't come naturally.'

I thought for a bit. 'Well, my dad tries. He's a feeb, but he tries. It's Mum who really gets me. She never puts me first. Work yes, J yes, but never me.' I was getting quite worked up.

'What was her family like?'

'Her mum died when she was about twelve and—'

'Ah! Don't you think that's your answer . . . ?'

'Donald, that's too pat! And anyway, what's with all this psychology stuff? Why can't I just hate my mother like any normal teenage girl . . . '

'Because it's not in character. You're far too sw—'

But he didn't finish his sentence. He stood up, out of range, and skipped about a bit. 'Leg's gone to sleep,' he told me, by way of explanation. So much for hugs. I felt confused. Donald had touched a nerve, a real point of dissatisfaction in my life. I felt exposed. I couldn't think of anything to say. I wanted to tell him I really liked him, that I thought he was fantastic. I wanted to talk about life, the world, the future, our future, but we'd talked about my mother and I felt cheated. Bloody mother. Always spoiling things.

'Hannah?' He sat down on the edge of the bunker. His feet were swinging somewhere round by my nose.

'Yes?' I shifted so that I could look up at him.

'Do you ever write any music?'

'Only what I've done at school. I prefer making it up as I go along. Why?'

'I've got an idea for a song. Well, I'm not much

good on the words but I think the tune might be OK. Can I play it to you some time?'

'Of course. If we ever get out of here!'

He peered at his watch. 'It must be getting on for six. I could do with something to eat. I need a pee too.'

'Thank you for sharing that with me.' I needed a loo, too, but I wasn't about to say so. 'There's plenty of food around!'

'And not a bite to eat. Actually, I bet there's some ice-cream!' He jumped down from the bunker and started to lift the lids on the freezers. 'Over here! Wow! They've got Magnums and Feasts and things. Want one?'

I stood up on my cramped legs and went over to have a look. The light inside the freezer lit up his intent face. He looked all excited, like a little boy. 'Here, bet you'd like a white Magnum,' he said, handing me one.

'Yes. How did you know?'

'I got you sussed, kid!' he said, closing the lid and tearing the wrapper off his lolly with a flourish. 'Ah. What do we do with the evidence?' He crumpled it up. 'Pockets I suppose. You just seem like . . . My sister Fiona likes them, that's why.'

We stood leaning against the freezer with our lollies for a bit. It was good having something to do. I was catching plenty of the amazing smiles (well, gleaming teeth in the darkness) and loads of chat, but nothing more. *Hannah!* I gave myself a mental slap on the wrist. I was in love with Donald. But I had spent the first few days either avoiding him or giving him a hard time. He had no reason to like me. No other boy had ever fancied me as far as I knew. He was probably really hacked off. Fancy being stuck in a cold store with Duck! I could imagine him telling the others after. How much more fun to be stuck in a cold store with Adela, say . . .

I jumped when he said, 'I suppose Adela's master-class is over by now.'

'I'm sorry,' I said. 'Kevin made you miss it because of me.'

'Kevin didn't want me there. Nothing to do with you.'

'I thought Kevin liked Jessa,' I said, and wished I hadn't.

'He does,' said Donald bluntly. 'But he's fascinated by Adela.'

'Him and all the others,' I said, and he didn't bother to contradict me.

He carried on as if I'd never interrupted. 'If the masterclass is over they might start to miss us soon. Kevin had this idea we might go for a swim if the weather cleared up. You ought to come, you know.'

'Some time,' I said vaguely. Funny, I'd been so

positive Don knew all about *why* I hadn't been swimming. It occurred to me for the first time that he hadn't a clue, that he didn't even know who I was in Boots, let alone what I had in my basket. Why should he have cared anyway? Maybe I should review events in a different light . . .

'I think we should go and sit by the door again,' said Don. 'Look, Hannah, I'm really sorry about all this. It's my fault we're locked in here.'

I wanted to say that I didn't mind at all. That having him to myself was everything I could have wished for. But all I could manage was a wry-sounding, 'I suppose it isn't exactly *my* fault . . . ' There was no answer to that, so we squatted down by the door again in silence. Neither of us said a word for several minutes. My mind was ablaze with 'what is he thinking?' thoughts, and I was taut as a wire with trying not to brush against him.

I could sense his agitation. He stood up suddenly and knocked me off balance as I sat back on my heels. He put out a hand to steady me, a firm, gentle hand on my arm. I thought for an agonising moment that perhaps he was going to hold me, but then I realised he was just being his caring self. Aagh.

'Sorry,' he said. 'Didn't mean to send you flying – Hey! Listen . . . ' We could hear definite sounds of people approaching, scrunchy gravel sorts of noises, chatter and laughter.

'That laugh sounds like Gemma—' I suddenly thought about how it would be when someone discovered us. What would they think? Kevin or Sam would know the situation, but what about Adela, or even Jessa, or one of the girls? What would rumour-monger Max make of it? What conclusions would people draw when they knew we'd spent over an hour alone together, or worse still, what if it was one of the staff and we were caught, knicker haul and all?

'How can we get their attention?' He seemed to lose his nerve. 'D'you think we should shout?'

'We could bang on the door,' I said. We both banged, furiously. But to no avail. They were obviously going in to supper, but no one heard us.

Despondent, we crouched down by the door again. As if to raise our spirits, a ray of sunlight crept under the door. Donald looked at his watch again. 'It's quarter to seven. We've been here nearly two hours . . . My, how time flies when you're enjoying yourself.'

But he didn't say it as if he meant it, and my heart was plummeting at the thought of how I had wasted the opportunities of two whole hours. All I wanted to do was to find out if he liked me, and I hadn't a clue how to go about it.

'They'll be coming back again in a while. They must have missed us at supper. Kev will expect me to go swimming with him. I'm starving—' He paused to draw breath and laughed at himself. 'Sorry—'

'Stop apologising! Neither of us can help it about being locked in. Actually, this reminds me of when I'd been naughty when I was little, and my parents used to shut me in my bedroom and say I couldn't go down and eat with them until I'd apologised. It's that same mixture of guilt and rebelliousness and – hunger.'

'We mustn't talk about being hungry. It just makes you hungrier. God! No one ever shut me in anywhere when I was a kid. They were all far too indulgent.'

'Lucky you.'

'I dunno. It made boarding-school all the more of a shock. Kids don't forgive you for anything. And you can't go rushing to Mummy. The trouble with boarding-school is that you just have to get on with people. I've thought about this a lot. Day kids can go home, sound off and be thoroughly nasty if need be and, generally, their parents know they're just letting off steam. But if you're a boarder it's all too easy to be really evil just once and you've got a reputation to live down ever after. I think I cottoned on to that very quickly. Survival. So as a result it takes people a long time to find out what I'm really thinking. It's something that gets in the way of being spontaneous.'

Was he trying to tell me something? 'Just think how much you'll enjoy being 'orrible from now on.

No more being sent to Coventry in the "dorm" . . .
You can take out the frustrations of the day on your
parents or the cat, and everyone'll go on loving you
just the same.' Scary mum and me both.

'Yeah, s'pose so.' He was distracted again. 'You
know that song I was talking about?'

'The one you've written? What's the accompani-
ment?'

'Oh, it's still in my head at the moment. I suppose I
could play it on the sax until I work the words out.
But – when could you listen to it?'

'Don! We're stuck in here! You can hum it to me if
you want!'

'Now? Oh God, no. No way! I need a keyboard for
security. I really only sing in the shower. Kevin's our
singing boy—'

'OK, OK!' I had heard him singing harmonies and
at least he could sing in tune, but he clearly didn't
want to now. 'Whenever. I mean, once we're out of
here. Whenever.' I was repeating myself. I couldn't
work out what sort of answer he wanted.

'Tomorrow evening?'

'As I said, whenever.'

'I don't know if it's any good, you see.'

'Don, whenever you want to play it I'm happy to
listen. OK?'

'Thanks.'

So what was all that about?

'I can hear them again!' We both leant with our ears to the door. 'Let's shout this time, and bang,' I said. There went the voices and the laughter. It was so tantalising. We could even hear Kevin saying, 'Who's coming for a swim then?' and a general smattering of replies.

'KEVIN!' we both yelled. 'WE'RE LOCKED IN HERE!' and we banged vigorously on the door. But they went past.

'I really don't believe this,' said Don. 'It calls for another ice-cream I think. Want one?'

'No thanks.' I was desperate to get out, to get to a loo, to get out of my uncomfortable swimsuit that I'd been wearing all day. 'Hang on! I think they might be coming back!' I could hear laughter outside.

It was Kevin! 'Oi! Donnie lad. What you up to in there?'

And Jessa. 'Duck! Are you in there?'

And Max. 'Donald! Duck! Donald! Duck!' followed by lots of silly Donald Duck quacking noises.

'We're locked in!' we both shouted.

'You'll need a key!'

'Don't panic!' came Kevin's voice. More laughter. 'We could break this padlock. Tell you what would be better . . . Jessa, do you reckon you could charm someone into giving us the key? Try the caretaker's house by the old building.'

'OK, Kevin.'

I smiled to myself. That's my Jessa. Anything to please Kevin. Kevin and Max came back to the door. It didn't sound as if anyone else was out there. 'You two OK?'

'Hungry!' said Don.

'Anything to be alone with a woman!' Max bellowed.

'Shut it Max. We don't want everyone to hear us,' said Kevin.

Yeah, shut it Max, I thought.

'Jessa's been really quick,' Kevin reported. 'She's running back already, and it looks as though she's holding a bunch of keys.'

'I wonder what she told him?' I asked Donald.

'Do we care?'

I cared a lot about what people said when we got out. Clearly Don didn't.

We heard a lot more sniggering and the sound of someone sorting keys. Then one was fitted in the padlock. I could have cried when I heard it snap apart. The doors were wrenched open from outside and sunlight flooded into the cold store that had been our prison. Jessa linked her arm in mine. She was full of her good deed. 'The caretaker was a real sweetie. Said he wouldn't ask any questions, but to get the key back straightaway. And why not have an ice-cream each while we were about it. I couldn't believe it . . . '

Meanwhile I was aware of Max running rings round all of us saying, 'Nearly two hours in the storeroom! I don't know Don. You're a quiet one!'

And then I caught sight of Kevin raising his eyebrows at Don and Don clutching the black plastic sack and mouthing – 'I wish!'

'Go on,' Jessa was saying, walking me away from the boys. 'You jammy woman. Tell me what happened! I want to know all the details.'

'Oh, nothing,' I said, 'Nothing at all!'

'I don't believe you,' said Jessa.

'Well, you'd better, because it's the truth,' I said. But to myself I thought *I wish*.

Nine

Gemma got up first as usual on Monday. Adela was spark out and Jessa and I were still lying in bed talking about yesterday's events. Our first problem the night before had been over the redistribution of the knickers. Then Jessa had had the brilliant idea of putting them all in a laundry basket and leaving it somewhere conspicuous. She managed to do this completely openly without anyone seeing her. Somehow no one expected Jessa to be up to anything. It worked a treat. Word got around and everyone went and sorted out their own knickers.

Jessa had definitely rescued me in my hour of need but she hadn't let up about Donald and me being locked up together and whether or not we fancied one another. I found I was protesting and then wondering whether I was protesting too much. She made me very flustered. I kept thinking how differently Sophie would have handled this situation. Every now and then Jessa gave me a break and waxed lyrical about the possibility of being locked in with Kevin. Once when she'd fixed me with a piercing gaze and said, 'Now, look me in the eye and deny that you fancy Donald,' I'd nearly caved in. In some ways it would have been lovely to share my secret with someone, but I was terrified of making a fool of myself. I couldn't risk it.

She was at it again this morning. 'Just imagine if you *had* fancied Donald. Nearly two hours alone with him. Or if he'd fancied you. I suppose,' she added, somewhat thoughtlessly, 'he can't have fancied you or he would have tried it on. He had plenty of opportunity.' I'd considered this possibility. But I'd also thought about the various conversations we'd had and about what he might have been trying to say rather than what he actually had said. On the whole I felt hopeful, so it wasn't great to hear Jessa's views on the matter.

It was even less great to hear Adela mumbling thickly, 'Butt out, Jessa. Hannah doesn't rate Donald's sex appeal. She told me that ages ago, didn't you Duck?'

I didn't know how to reply. So I just pretended I hadn't heard and went off for a shower.

If I'd thought Jessa was bad, I'd reckoned without Max. He was already having a go at Donald when we turned up for sectionals. 'Weyhey Donald! Here comes your ice maiden. Two hours! Kuh! Two hours and he says nothing happened—'

'Shut up, Max,' said Donald apparently unperturbed. 'Hi Duck! Sax lesson after lunch then?' But underneath the bravado he was giving me the worried glance that I was coming to recognise.

'Yeah, great,' I said, ignoring Jessa's pointed looks and Max's muttered 'Sax after sex' comments. I tried to focus on the sectional.

We all ended up at the same lunch table, so of course my forthcoming saxophone lesson was up for general review. In some ways the openness of it all made it easier to handle. I found I could even pretend that music *was* all it was about. That's the way Donald was playing it, because that's the way it was for him. He didn't have to pretend, I realised sadly.

'OK,' he said, when lunch was over. 'Sax masterclass time, Duck.'

'Now this I must see,' said Kevin, attaching himself to us.

'And me!' said Jessa and Adela together.

'Oh no,' said Don. 'This is one small practice room. Three will be a crowd, five would be an orgy . . .'

I was quite glad to have Kevin as a chaperone. Maybe Don was too. He detached the head from his saxophone and showed me how to blow on it. He made the right embouchure with his mouth and made me copy it, so we spent a lot of time mouthing at each other. Kevin found this all very amusing and kept saying that he felt like a gooseberry. But he didn't go away. Once I could make a decent sound Don assembled the sax again. He was about to put it to his lips when I realised that the mouthpiece must be covered in my spit. 'Er – do you want me to wipe it?' I asked, embarrassed as usual.

'Nah,' said Don. 'I'm sure it'll taste lovely,' and proceeded to show me how to finger the notes. 'There. You try. It's just the same as the flute, I don't think you'll have a problem.' He handed me the sax again. I felt self-conscious as I put it back to my lips. It seemed a terribly intimate thing to do, but I had no choice and Don was concentrating on teaching me to play *Take Five*. I thought I did quite well for a first-timer, and so did he.

'What d'you think, Kev?' he asked.

Kevin was less than enthusiastic. 'We-ell . . .'

'Kevin!' Donald wasn't having it. 'This lady has never picked up a sax before. If she can do that now, by Saturday we'll have a pro on our hands!'

'OK, OK!' Kevin laughed. 'If you say so! Come on both of you. Time for the afternoon session.'

'I'll see you there. Thanks for the lesson,' I said, and made a dash for it. I needed some fresh air, and the chance to savour the taste of Don's lips. Wow.

I met up with Jessa coming down from the girls' block. 'Well?' she asked. 'How was it?'

'Cool,' I said, giving nothing away.

'Can I come and listen this evening? We're not having a quintet rehearsal today. I'd like to be near Kevin without Adela for once. That girl is driving me nuts!'

'Yes, sure,' I said, 'So long as you realise I'm only a beginner and don't go all critical like Kevin did.'

'Oh, I'm sure he didn't mean it!' Jessa leapt to his defence. 'Kevin would never be unkind. I mean, you should hear how sweet he is to Adela, even when she's being irritating as hell. Everyone else is wincing, but he's still nice as pie.'

'I wouldn't call that kind, exactly—' I started, but Jessa came down on me like a ton of bricks.

'Well, it couldn't possibly be for any other reason.

Everyone knows she's just a little slapper who happens to be very good at the violin.'

I kept quiet, but I wasn't so sure that that was how guys saw Adela, or, if they did, that they minded in the least.

After supper I set off for the music block with Donald. I was beginning to relax with him. It wasn't difficult when he was being all enthusiastic. If I suppressed my romantic notions and assumed that he had none of his own it was perfectly possible to be good mates – because he was so, well, nice! Jessa and Kevin and Sam followed behind.

'I meant to try out my song on you after lunch,' said Donald. 'But I didn't really want to with Kevin around. Perhaps we'll get a chance later on. Would you mind?'

Before I had a chance to answer, Adela came rushing over to join us. 'Can I come, too?' she asked. 'Quartet's cancelled. I'm longing to hear you and Kevin doing jazz, Donnie. Are you sure you don't need a violinist? Or female vocals?' and she caught hold of Don's arm and skipped alongside him, ignoring me completely. Perhaps it was time I stopped defending that girl. I fell back to be with Jessa, just as Kevin strode forward to be with Donnie and Adela. Jessa and I exchanged snarls. For once I could understand just how she was feeling.

I wasn't sure how I felt about playing in front of an audience. The first three pieces were OK. Adela mercifully kept her mouth shut, though Jessa was clapping away after each one. The lads were being complimentary, so I suppose Adela couldn't be too critical. Then it was time for my saxophone debut.

'We'll take it really slow, OK?' said Don. 'In fact, you go at a pace you can handle, Duck, and we'll follow.'

Adela started muttering, 'Good job we don't all need that sort of treatment,' but she was drowned out as we got going. I managed to get through it, but I made an awful lot of squeaks and odd noises along the way. Kevin shot me some amused looks, and so did Jessa, but Adela just creased up with giggles. It was really offputting. I wanted Kevin to shut her up, but in fact it was Don who had a go at her.

'This is only the second time Duck has played a saxophone, Adela. And she's doing bloody well. If you can't be sympathetic, bog off. We need to rehearse.'

'I'll say,' said Adela, stung. I could see that for once she felt awkward. She didn't like being dismissed. So she went on the charm offensive. 'Sorry. Honestly I am. I didn't mean to laugh. You're all sounding great. Really,' and she pulled the sleeves of her jumper down over her hands and wrapped her arms around her legs, settling in. Hatred was oozing out of

Jessa. She was ominously silent during this exchange.

We played *Take Five* a couple more times. I felt a little more confident, but not a whole lot. Kevin and Sam packed their gear away. As Sam left, Don caught my eye. 'Hang about,' he said. 'Don't forget my song.' I wasn't sure how this was going to work. But I'd forgotten the Kevin magnetism. When he moved towards the door Adela and Jessa followed him as one.

Don laughed. 'What's his secret? Sure you don't mind listening to this Duck? I wouldn't ask, but . . . ' He trailed off.

'Get on with it! Are you going to sing?'

'No. I know what the song's about, but I haven't sorted the words yet.' He looked away.

'Go on!' I sat on the floor by the keyboard.

He smoothed out a sheet of manuscript paper and started to play. I could feel him looking down at me, but I didn't dare to look up. It was a sweet, romantic tune. It made me think of rain and flowers. It was beautiful. I felt that Don was trying to tell me something with it that he couldn't say in words. The song drew to a close. I sat with my forehead on my knees, overwhelmed, just longing for him to come over and put his arms round me—

The door crashed open and Adela and Jessa stormed in screaming at each other. I stood up, shocked. They were heading for me. 'Girls! Girls!' said Donald nervously.

'Tell her, Hannah!' Jessa was shouting. 'Tell her to leave Kevin alone. He doesn't like her following him around—'

'Tell *her*,' shrieked Adela, 'that Kevin is a lot more interested in someone like me than a sad nun like her!'

'I don't believe this,' I said. '*I* don't know what Kevin wants, but this is ridiculous! Calm down!'

'I'll be off then,' said Don, with an apologetic smile at me.

'I'll come with you,' said Adela, attaching herself to him like a limpet. Alarm bells should have rung at that point, but Jessa was claiming all my attention.

They left. 'Do you *know* what she did?' Jessa was still blazing.

'Tell me. I don't think anything Adela did would surprise me any more.'

'Well. The three of us, Kevin, me and Adela, all came down from the music block together after we'd left you. Kevin was talking to me and Adela didn't like that at all. And she was so – so blatant. Do you know, Duck, she just came up and grabbed his arm and said, "Kevin, come with me, there's something I want to show you," or something corny like that. Can you believe it? More to the point, he *went*! Like a little dog. She said "Bye Jessa, Kevin's coming with me now, aren't you Kev?" There didn't seem to be much I could do so I just went back towards the dormitory. But I decided to follow them and there was Adela trying to snog him! I could see he wasn't really happy about it – he kept pulling away, and saying things like "Hang on Adela! I think there's been a misunderstanding" and stuff. So, I'm ashamed to say, I hung around to listen. And Adela went on and on, pressing herself up against him, stroking his hair, putting her hands in his back pockets – you know the sort of thing. She was really trying to seduce him. And she kept saying, "Oh come on Kevin. You know you fancy me!" The way she was going on I'm surprised he resisted, but he did. He suddenly pushed her away quite roughly and shouted, "Look Adela! Stop it! You're making a fool of yourself. I don't fancy you. And—" Then they walked on, back in this direction again. It was so frustrating! I was dying to hear what he was going to say next! Anyway, I decided to go round and inter- cept them. And that's when I heard Adela still saying, "Oh come *on* Kev!" . . . And I just flipped. I walked up to them and told her to leave him alone! Kevin looked really shocked, and started to back away and that's when I dragged Adela over to you. I don't know what got into me. Sheer jealousy I think!'

All the fight had gone out of Jessa. 'Sorry, Duck,' she said weakly. 'I really don't know what came over me. Arguing with that *child*, it's pointless.' She looked slyly at me. 'And what did we barge in on, eh? You and Donald alone again?'

I told her the truth. 'He wanted me to listen to a song he's writing. He's shy about it.'

'Wish Kevin wanted me to listen to his songs. I love him so much, Duck. You can't imagine how it feels.'

I thought I could.

Ten

We didn't bother to wake Adela in the morning. Jessa had calmed down. It was a gorgeous day with blue holiday skies and we wanted to get out there. I felt blissfully confident about Donald, and what's more I was looking forward to going in the pool at last. Things were definitely looking up. There might even be a romance in the offing to surprise the others with when I got home.

Everyone was affected by the good weather. We threw the doors open for the sectionals and caught snatches of the other groups rehearsing. It sounded like a mad party.

Donald was giving me a quick sax lesson after

lunch and then Kevin was organising everyone for a swim. Whole orchestra rehearsal was starting half an hour later than usual, so we'd be able to make the most of the afternoon sun. My lesson was fun. After yesterday's raw beginnings I was getting the hang of it. Donald was very professional this time and just gave me hints rather than demonstrations. Then he sat down at the keyboard and we vamped through *Take Five* together. I even did some pretty cool improvising. He grinned at me and said we made beautiful music together, though he didn't look me in the eye as he said it.

On the way out he asked me if Adela was OK. 'Yes,' I said. 'Why shouldn't she be?'

He hesitated. 'Well, she seemed to be in quite a state yesterday evening. We – she seemed very upset about Kevin.'

'She was fine when I last saw her,' I said, and thought no more of the conversation.

Jessa and Gemma were gathering up their swimming things from our room. 'Kevin's been organising again,' said Jessa excitedly. 'Apparently he's found all these inflatables – turtles and sharks and lilos.' I had my new bikini on. 'Wow, Duck, you're really brown. When did you get your tan?'

'Still left over from the south of France last summer.' I looked down at myself. I wasn't really brown but at least I wasn't completely white. I can't swim in my glasses so I decided to leave them behind. 'Are we off then?'

The pool was heaving. I slipped in for a couple of lengths. It was blissfully cool but a bit of an obstacle course. I kept bumping into squealing kids on giant spotty things. Jessa called out to me. 'I've bagged a couple of lilos, Duck. Come out and sunbathe with me. I want to borrow your suntan lotion.' I hauled myself out and blindly located Jessa and two red lilos. 'Over here,' she called, seeing me peering at people.

We settled ourselves in for the afternoon. We had suntan lotion, books, bottles of water, even some crisps. For the first time it really felt as if we were on holiday.

Our lilos became a sort of base camp. Gemma, Max, Helen, Josie and the Horns pitched up alongside us. Kevin, Don and Adela had some elaborate waterfight going on. I was far too lazy to want to join in. Then Max and the Horns went to join in the battle and Adela came and sat near by. It was obvious she thought that we were where the action was, but she didn't want to sit too close to Jessa. I was peering closely at my book and just then I really didn't care.

I could hear Kevin chatting to Jessa. They were sitting together on her lilo. I shaded my eyes and turned to speak to them. 'Hi! How's the battle going?'

'Hannah!' said Kevin, surprised. 'I didn't recognise you—'

'—without your clothes on!' Jessa finished for him.

'Nice – erm – bikini,' he finished lamely.

'It's like Brighton beach here,' said Jessa. 'And, oh God, Adela is going for the all-over tan again!'

'Now?' I turned over to look in Adela's direction. It wasn't quite as bad as Jessa made out. She was lying on her front, reading. One of the boys was pouring suntan lotion into his hand about to anoint her, I couldn't really see who.

'Good old Donald!' I heard Kevin say. I peered shortsightedly in Adela's direction again. The man with the oil was indeed Donald. But Kevin was talking to me again. 'You look great Hannah,' he said appreciatively, and smiled at me with those melting eyes. I suffered a major wibble. 'Come for a swim, cool off a bit,' and he reached out a hand to pull me to my feet. He didn't let go either but carried on pulling me to the water's edge.

'Remember I'm blind without my glasses!' I yelled.

'Don't worry! I'm looking where I'm going! Jump now!' And we both landed up in the pool.

We splashed around for a bit but the pool was still crowded. Once I'd cooled off I decided I'd rather be sunbathing. 'I'm getting out again,' I told him. 'Time for a bit of heavy-duty basting and roasting I think.'

'Good idea,' said Kevin. 'I'll lead you back again,' and he grabbed my hand.

'Over here!' Jessa waved and we picked our way towards the lilos.

Jessa sat up and moved over to accommodate Kevin again. I flopped down on my front. 'Someone do my back?' I asked and held out the lotion. I had meant Jessa, so I was slightly surprised when Kevin took it and said, 'Yes, I will.'

I could hear the bewilderment in Jessa's voice as she said, 'Will you do me too?'

'Oh. Yes. All right then. I'll do you both.'

Kevin and the suntan lotion was an experience not to be forgotten. I'll freely admit it's the closest *I've* ever been to having sex. God. When I'd had oil firmly massaged into every centimetre of skin on my back (and thank God I didn't have spots there) I turned my head to see how Jessa was enjoying her turn. As I thought, she was in heaven. Then I turned to look the other way. Donald appeared to be asleep but Adela, I could tell even from this distance, held us in a steely gaze. Kevin lay on the other side of Jessa. They were chatting in a desultory sort of way. I couldn't hear what they were saying, and anyway my addled brain was drifting idly between Don's song and Kevin's massage and Don's smile and the taste of Don's lips . . . Jessa was too hot and got up to cool off in the water. Kevin slid on to her lilo.

'How're you doing Hannah?'

'Fine.'

'That's good.'

The time for the afternoon rehearsal drew closer. No one seemed to want to move – we were like beached seals. Jessa stood up – she did look lovely in her lilac bikini, all slender with soft curves – 'Come on Duck. I want a shower before the rehearsal.' I certainly didn't want to walk out of there alone. So we picked our way through the bodies again, reaching Adela just as she was fumbling with the clasp of her bikini behind her back, and Don just as he was offering to do it for her.

'Tart!' said Jessa as she dragged me away. 'Still, thank God she's turned her attentions to Don. Good job you don't fancy him, isn't it!'

I didn't like it one bit. Donnie was mine. I excused him on all fronts of course. He was just being nice to Adela. He felt sorry for her. I hadn't been there. I'd been with Kevin.

Oooh. There must be an explanation.

I went into the rehearsal. Don leant over. 'OK for jazz practice after supper, Duck?' He'd washed his hair. I could smell its clean scent.

'Sure,' I said. Please God let everything be all right. There didn't seem to be any major change in Don's behaviour. But then I had no proof that he felt anything special for me anyway. All I had were my feelings for him – that I'd kept to myself.

Adela's concerto took up the second half of the rehearsal. It was coming on really well. At those moments, when the notes soared above us or dipped below or sang out alone, she was ours and I could forgive her anything.

Kevin was paying me a lot of attention. This was a totally new experience for me and I didn't know how to handle it. When he came up to Jessa and me after the rehearsal I assumed it was to talk to Jessa, but it soon became apparent that it was me he was focusing on. It was the 'Hi Hannah – oh, and hi Jessa,' sort of thing. And, 'Do you two do *every*thing together?' After supper, when it was time for our jazz practice, he practically dragged me away from Jessa, saying 'Have a good toot, Jessa. Come on Hannah, Donnie tells me you're getting brilliant. Can't wait to hear you.' Jessa cast me a reproachful look, but there wasn't a lot I could do.

Our practice was really great. My sax playing had come on in leaps and bounds in only two days. I felt mighty proud of myself, but the best part was that the guys seemed proud of me too. I began to feel like one of the lads. Not that Kevin was going to let me. He commented on the clothes I was wearing, talked at length about how good I'd looked without my glasses, told the others to see how cool I looked when I played sax. I really couldn't believe it.

We emerged from the practice room into a beautiful romantic summer evening, the sort I seemed to have spent with either Jessa or Adela so far. The sky still glowed pink and the scented jasmine flowers shone out like stars. I waited a little, letting Kevin and Sam go ahead so that I could walk with Don. Tomorrow was the day of our outing to Cambridge and the instrument workshops. I knew he'd been there before and I wanted to ask him about it. He came out humming. 'Don?' I longed to put my hand in his and wander off into the sunset with him. He looked down at me and my stomach lurched.

But I never got any further. Kevin had come back to us at the same time as Jessa and the others in her quintet spilled out of their practice room. And that was unfortunate because Jessa arrived on the scene at the same time as Kevin was saying, 'You are coming on the outing tomorrow, aren't you Hannah? It will be so cool to get away from this place for the day.'

'Yes, we're coming,' said Jessa, linking her arm in mine and giving me a funny look. 'See you on the coach, guys,' she said as she steered me away from them. So here I was about to spend the evening with Jessa again.

But Jessa had fire in her eyes. She walked me firmly to the bench under the chestnut tree and sat me down. She checked that no one else was around. In fact most of them had gone up to the dormitories. 'OK, Ms Duck,' she said a tad fiercely. 'Tell me. What precisely is going on between you and Kevin? It hasn't escaped my notice that he has been buttering you up nonstop since the moment he saw you in a bikini. So what's it all about?'

'Honest, Jess, I don't know myself. I promise I haven't done a thing to encourage him! I agree with you that he's totally gorgeous, but he's not really my type. Anyway it's—' I stopped myself. I had come so close to telling Jessa about Don so many times I almost forgot that she didn't know. Perhaps now was the time to tell her. But she wasn't really listening.

'I don't understand it. I could have killed Adela last night for muscling in, and I ought to want to kill you, but it's just so weird. I mean, you have to admit, he seems to chat you up in front of me, almost on purpose. But why? Why now? I really thought he liked me, Duck. I really thought I was beginning to get somewhere. And with Adela, well, I can dismiss her because I don't think much of her, but you! That's different!'

I decided the time had come to lay my cards on the table. 'Jessa. Listen to me. For what it's worth, I'm not the slightest bit interested in Kevin. I – the only person I'm interested in is Don. There. I've said it now.'

Jessa was gawping at me. 'So I was right all along. I *knew* you and Donald had something going, you sneaky thing. I could tell he fancied you rotten. *And* you lied about the cold store episode. Duck! You are a dark horse!'

'No, Jessa. No. We haven't got anything going at all. That's the problem. I'm crazy about him but I don't think he's the slightest bit interested in me, not like that, anyway. In fact he seems a bit keen on Adela now.'

'Cow,' hissed Jessa, not for the first time.

'So. I haven't got a clue what Kevin's up to. I thought you two were getting on really well too. I think it's wait-and-see time, Jessie-baby. All will be revealed . . .'

'Yes. Perhaps by the time we get back tomorrow we'll understand a bit more.' She gave me a hug. 'Oooh, Duck! I'd so love you and Donald to get together. You're perfect for one another. Teehee! Donald Duck!' and she ran off to the dormitory block with me in hot pursuit.

Eleven

Another gorgeous day. Our room was a whirl of strappy dresses and short tops, shorts, short skirts and sandals. Even Jessa and Adela weren't glaring at one another as we discussed what to wear on a hot day out. We picked up our packed lunches after breakfast and bundled onto the coach.

The plan was this: coach to the workshops of the Instrument-makers' Guild just outside Cambridge, where we would see the whole range of musical instruments being made and repaired by hand. It sounded boring, but Don had been before and said it was worth it, if only to meet the flute-maker, George Hooper, a real craftsman of the old school, who made some of the most expensive flutes in the world. Then picnic by the Cam. Then the choice of an afternoon on the river or looking round colleges, with a bit of time for shopping afterwards. Supper was being laid on in one of the college canteens and then there was a short concert in Kings College Chapel before the coach took us back again. They'd been to Brighton one year, Oxford another. Parents obviously approved of University towns for days out. Personally I'd have preferred Chessington with the juniors, but with weather like this, the river trip sounded good. As Kevin had said, it would be great to get away from the course for a day.

Jessa was keeping very close to Kevin as we boarded the coach. And Kevin was keeping quite close to me, while I was looking out for Donnie – though I couldn't see him. Kevin sat by a window and Jessa dived in beside him. I sat across the aisle from her, but then Adela told me to shove up to the window and ended up there instead. At least if Adela was sitting next to me she wasn't sitting next to Don. I saw him at last, definitely one of the stragglers, along with Sam. They were deep in conversation and sat down together, still talking, near the front, along with Max and the Horns, Josie and Helen. Gemma was also at the front, sitting with Miss Claggan, but that was Gemma for you.

Adela grinned slyly over at me and cast a glance towards Kevin. 'I'd say you're in, there, Ducks. Poor old Jessa.'

'What makes you think I want to be?' I really didn't want to spend the coach journey being goaded by Adela, but I couldn't let her get away with it.

'Weyhey! I saw him applying the suntan lotion by the pool yesterday, Duck! And I have to say, I was almost too embarrassed to watch!'

'Oh come off it. He put some on Jessa as well!' I was going to add something about Donald doing the same for her, but I was scared of giving myself away. Fortunately for me, the coach lurched into action at that moment. 'We're off! Great! Today should be cool.'

'Bit educational, if you ask me,' said Adela. 'Wish we could have gone to Chessington with the little ones. Still, going in a punt could be good. I've always fancied that. Bit like a gondola in Venice. Not that I've ever done that. Too touristy.'

'Isn't punting on the Cam touristy?'

'Well, I'll be a tourist there, won't I?' Adela leant across Jessa to Kevin. 'You'll come in a punt with us, won't you, Kevin?'

Jessa looked up crossly, but Kevin smiled and said, 'Possibly, Adela, very possibly.'

I looked out of the window at the unfolding countryside. It was already hot. The cornfields were bleached pale gold and ready for harvest. The trees looked dark by contrast and cast dark shadows. There was a heat haze already. Constable harvest weather. Picnic weather! I wanted to share it all with Don. Damn it, why wasn't he with us? As if she'd overheard my thoughts, Adela suddenly said, 'Poor old Don. I tried to cheer him up yesterday, but I think I'm going to have to look after him today as well.'

'You what?' I couldn't believe what I was hearing. But I checked myself. I wanted to hear what Adela was going to say next without giving my feelings away. 'Sorry Adela, I hadn't noticed Donald was upset about anything.'

'Well, you wouldn't have done, would you? Not with the gorgeous Kevin all over you. I mean who would notice droopy Donald with cute Kevin around?'

'What are you saying, Adela? I told you—' I lowered my voice so Kevin couldn't hear—'I didn't necessarily want . . . '

' 'Course you do! And that's what I said to Donald when I told him not to make a fool of himself over you. I said you'd told me you really didn't fancy him. He looked so upset that I thought it would soften the blow a bit if I told him it was because there was someone else –' she nodded in Kevin's direction, '– you know.'

My jaw must have dropped as I looked at her in sheer horror. 'Adela,' I said, 'Did you do this just to spite Jessa?'

She looked at me coolly. Her eyes looked slightly out of focus. 'No, no,' she said vaguely. 'I admit I was upset about Kevin leading me on and then letting me down, but then of course I realised *he* must like someone else. He couldn't have had any other reason for not wanting *me*, could he? But I was pretty unhappy that night after Jessa had shrieked at me, and Donald was so sweet and kind when we came away from the music block. And he did look a bit as if he was mooning over you when we burst in on you. And I *know* you don't think he's sexy, Hannah, you must remember telling me so yourself.'

I must have been glaring at her. She said, 'I was doing you a *favour* for God's sake. Jessa can look after herself, but I was trying to help you.'

I opened my mouth to speak, but no sound came out. Poor Donald. Poor me. So many things explained. But what was Adela playing at with Donald?

'Don't worry, I'll look after poor Donald this afternoon,' she said. And she gave me her impish look. 'I've *always* thought he was fit . . .'

I turned to look out of the coach window and took some deep breaths. This was like a bad dream. Donald thought I didn't fancy him. He thought I preferred Kevin. He must have told Kevin. He must have decided to show me that he didn't care. I glanced over at Jessa and Kevin. They were getting on fine. Kevin must have realised that I wasn't very rewarding . . . God what a mess. I felt completely helpless. Thanks Adela. Thanks a lot.

We arrived at the workshops. They were housed in a group of beautiful converted barns attached to a seventeenth-century farmhouse that was now the showroom. A river ran beneath a row of willows behind them. The barns were clustered round what was once the farmyard, now a tasteful carpark. More than thirty of us piled out of the coach. I looked for

Donald, but he was definitely keeping his distance. Sam, who I knew was interested in making instruments and genuinely enthusiastic about the visit, was talking with him. Jessa hustled Kevin as far from Adela as she could, so there I was again, with my old friend Adela. I had a sudden sharp sense of the day going horribly wrong.

We were organised into six groups to go round the six workshops. Needless to say, Adela and I weren't with either Jessa and Kevin or Donald and Sam. But we were with Helen and Josie and the Horns, which suited me fine. In our first workshop they were making harpsichords and clavichords. Sunlight slanted in onto the fragrant piles of woodshavings that surrounded the two craftsmen. The scene reminded me of a painting I'd seen once. Already the day seemed to be passing in a series of picture frames. I loved the little clavichord, with its black keys where the white keys on a piano are and pale wooden keys for the 'black' notes. When I touched the keys a soft silvery sound came out. Why can't my parents spend their money on something like this rather than the latest BMW? I carried on playing quietly as Adela chatted up one of the makers. I remembered some of the chords of Donald's flowers and rain song . . . the clavichord was such a private and personal instrument . . . I imagined him sitting down at the same gentle keyboard. It would suit him. Perhaps he'd know that his music had been played on it . . . Oh Donnie! What was I going to do?

It was time to move on. We went through guitars, woodwind instruments and brass before we arrived at the violin maker, Wolf Prosser. He worked alone on his violins. Prosser was a feisty old gentleman, who obviously did not appreciate gangs of schoolchildren interrupting him, and we were the fifth group that morning. We hung back slightly, scared to touch anything. But then Adela, impulsive as always, saw a finished violin lying in its plush case and picked it out. She tuned it. We looked on nervously, but the violin maker seemed not to notice and carried on working. Suddenly Adela broke into her Mendelssohn. Dwarfed by the ancient rafters of the sunny barn she played like an angel. The Horns and Josie and Helen – who of course had refrained from showing anything other than polite interest when they saw their own instruments being made – raised their eyebrows at one another, but I could feel the tears pricking as they always did when Adela worked her magic. And I thought of Donald, and I thought of the beautiful day, and the fiasco it was becoming, and the tears welled up, clouding my glasses. I wasn't the only one affected. Adela finished playing and laid the violin back in its case. The violin maker stood up and went over to her, his eyes glistening. He put a gnarled hand on her arm. 'My dear,' he said simply, 'thank you. For this I make violins.' And he went back to his bench.

Humbled, we crept on to the final workshop, where George Hooper made the famous Hooper flutes. He was a craftsman metalworker, wearing an apron and with his sleeves rolled up. 'Have a good look round,' he said. 'Ask me anything. And I've got some heads over there if you want a blow. Any of you flute-players?'

'She is.' They all pointed at me.

'You seem a nice careful girl. Here. This is a gold head. See what you make of it.'

I'd heard about gold flutes, but I'd never tried one. 'Give it a wipe. Lad from the last group blew a lot of germs into it. I wouldn't want you to catch any-thing!' He gave a raucous chuckle. I made an elabo-rate play of wiping the lip plate and blew. Wow. A gorgeous golden sound. 'See? It makes you all sound like Jimmy Galway!'

We thanked him and went out into the bright sunlight, the last group out. 'A quick look round the showroom, everyone,' Miss Claggan was saying. She looked at her watch, 'And then back on the coach. It's midday already – I expect you're all gasping for something to drink.'

Jessa came and found me. 'Did you try the gold flute head?' she asked. 'I did, and so did Donald. Amazing, wasn't it? Donald told Mr Hooper to make

sure you tried it. Oh, and I sorted Kevin out . . .
Tell you more later,' she said as Kevin came towards
us.

So Donald was definitely avoiding me. I wasn't
imagining it. Jessa, Kevin and I found a tree to sit
under for our picnic. But as soon as we were off the
coach Adela ran up to Donald and Sam, linked an
arm through each of theirs and steered them as far
away from us as possible. I could hear her starting to
tell them about trying out the Prosser violin. To her
credit she only told them about how wonderful it
was, not how her playing moved the maker himself
to tears, but then I never heard the end of the story
because they were so far away. Jessa and Kevin were
getting along really well. I found myself feeling
distinctly left out. It wasn't that they weren't nice to
me, just that it was definitely 'them' and me. And
there in the distance was Adela being all animated
and cute – pass the sick bag – with Donald and Sam, I
could tell. I gave up. I took my glasses off, and lay
back in the sun.

'You coming punting, Donnie lad?'

'Come on, Donald,' Jessa was saying. 'Come with
us on the river.'

I heard Adela. 'Nah. River's for tourists, isn't it
Don?' But I didn't hear his reply. It wasn't what Adela

had said before. I sat up and rubbed my eyes. Glasses back on. Ah, hello world.

'You'll come on a boat with us, won't you Duck?' Jessa asked me. But I was getting mixed messages here. Jessa's voice wasn't as imploring as her words. And her expression seemed to be saying 'Please let me have Kevin to myself . . . '

I looked at her hard and said hesitantly – 'I thought I might have a wander round the colleges.' I'd read her expression right. She didn't ask again.

So, colleges it was. I attached myself to the colleges party while the boating lot went off to the boatyard to hire boats. I looked around our group. It did not contain Don and Adela.

Swine.

King's College Cambridge is a beautiful place. So is Queen's College and so are Trinity College, St John's, Peterhouse, Pembroke, Clare – and any others you'd care to mention. They soon merged into one. The heat was merciless. My newish sandals started to give me blisters. My friends were all out on the cool river. Donald was with Adela and they had skived off somewhere, together. I didn't have anything else to do until six o'clock, unless I felt like shopping – which I didn't – and I didn't have anyone to do it with anyway. We were all meeting up at the Clare canteen at half-past five. Tea was being laid on there before evensong next door in King's College chapel at six-fifteen. I told the others I'd see them at Clare for tea. I bought a bottle of Evian and went back through King's to the river. I lay in the shade with my chin on my hands and feasted my eyes on the green water, and thought of the pre-Raphaelite painting of drowned Ophelia, and envied her.

At five-thirty I got up to go. The thought of food and the concert cheered me a little, but just then a rowing boat slid into view. The oars were shipped. Two people were in it. The rower had taken his shirt off. His passenger lay back against him, a bottle of wine to her lips, giggling. He bent his silky head to her dark curly one and said something that brought peals of laughter from her. I drew back into the shadow of the tree. I'd just seen Donald and Adela.

I don't remember much about what happened after that. Somehow I got through tea and the concert without crying too much or too obviously. Somehow I managed the journey home in the front of the coach without looking back. Somehow I got into bed without telling Jessa to stop going on about Kevin. Somehow I fell asleep. I didn't hear when Adela came in.

Twelve

I was crying in my dream. My mum was shouting at me and someone was looking on, Sophie maybe. I was saying please stop, I really hadn't meant to be naughty . . . I woke up, great sobs rasping from my chest. Thank God it was only a dream. But I was unhappy, still. Then I remembered. Donald and Adela. I sat up in a sweat. Adela! Where was she? She was there, asleep, her back towards me. And there were Gemma and Jessa. Everything was normal. Except that it wasn't. I had lost Donald. I'd never even had him, of course, but now I'd lost him. To Adela. I looked at her sleeping form, and slid back down under my covers, overwhelmed with misery. I found myself snivelling, tears and snot combining somewhere around my chin.

The most difficult thing to come to terms with was that I hadn't seen what was going on. Everything had been fine, brilliant, until Monday night, when Adela and Jessa had had their row over Kevin. And then Adela had left the music block with Donald and I hadn't even realised.

It didn't matter when it had begun. It had happened, and now Donald obviously despised me and had got it together with Adela in a big way – I winced at the memory of them in the boat together. And Kevin was definitely interested in Jessa. Perhaps I was too young for all this. Perhaps older people had a code that I didn't understand. Or it wasn't so much older people as just less innocent people who had a code. Perhaps that included Sophie and the others. Perhaps they all just saw me as sad and hopelessly immature.

The self-pity was really building now. I pulled the bedclothes up over my head and tried to cry quietly. I cried myself back to sleep.

The morning bell cut through another miserable dream. In this dream I was drowning. I fought my way out from under the duvet and looked around. Adela was sleeping through the bell as usual. Jessa and Gemma were going off to the shower together. Jessa was definitely looking bright-eyed and bushy-tailed this morning. I thought about the day ahead and tried to decide on a course of action. If I stayed in bed I'd have to face Adela. If I got up while Jessa and Gemma were in the shower and made a run for it I wouldn't have to face any of them. But where would I run to? I was bound to bump into someone. Of course, Jessa was the only one who knew what I felt about Donald. But I couldn't face seeing Donald, and certainly not if he was all over Adela. If I carried on as normal I would have to go through a sectional with

Donald and Jessa and possibly a sax lesson with Donald. It looked like the sort of day when everyone would head for the swimming pool and that certainly didn't appeal to me. And then whole group rehearsal and probably a jazz practice. Hmmm. I felt ghastly.

That was it. I felt really ill. I would send my apologies and stay in bed for the morning. I could probably cope with whole orchestra and even the jazz practice. After all, I was going to have to face Donald some time and it would be easier to act normal with lots of other people around. It wasn't as if *he* knew my feelings had changed from 'not fancying him'. He certainly wasn't to know I'd fallen in love with him. Only Jessa knew that.

And how had *Adela*, who didn't really care, managed to get off with him, when I hadn't?

Gemma came back into the dormitory. She saw me still in bed and came over. 'You all right, Hannah?'

I sounded suitably groggy. 'Not really,' I croaked. 'I think I'll stay in bed this morning. Could you ask Jessa to tell people? Thanks.' I snuggled down again. I heard Gemma whispering to Jessa not to wake me up again, I wasn't well and Jessa murmuring 'Poor thing.' I heard Gemma go over and talk to Adela and tell her to let me sleep and Adela grunting something in response. This was a good way out. Exhausted, I went back to dreaming.

*

'Hi Hannah. Are you OK?' Donald touched my arm as I pushed past him to my seat. Emotion had drained me and I still felt a bit wobbly. He was looking concerned. Huh.

'I'll live,' I said.

He leant across the other Hannah as I sat down. He was still looking concerned. Then I realised why. 'D'you think you'll be able to manage a jazz practice this evening? We need to spend as much time as we can rehearsing.'

Of course. Don't want to spoil the music. Don't want the precious jazz group to appear unrehearsed. I looked away. 'I'll be fine,' I said, concentrating on setting up my music on the stand. We were doing the Rimsky-Korsakov Variations and I had to concentrate on my piccolo solo. Thank God we were giving the Mendelssohn a rest. I don't think I could have borne Adela strutting her stuff just then. Jessa caught my eye. She gave me a 'that's ma girl!' smile as the conductor raised his baton, and I felt strengthened.

I needed all the strength I could get. In the break Adela bustled over to the flute section. 'Hi Duck. I thought you were ill! Don, darlin', come with me for a quick one. Smoke,' she added, as if she was shocking us all. She pulled him out of his seat and dragged him out, leaving a trail of rocking music stands in her wake.

Jessa took my arm. 'Let's go and grab a drink, Han. I've got things to tell you.'

The break was only twenty minutes. 'Forget the drink, let's just go for a walk.' It seemed strangely bright outside to my red puffy eyes. 'God Hannah, you look awful.'

We found a tree to sit under. I looked at Jessa expectantly. 'I'm happy for you, Jessa. Don't worry about me. I think I'm probably over Donald already. He and Adela deserve each other.'

'Like hell!' said Jessa. 'I always knew the cow was complicated, but I never quite knew how complicated. I'm only just beginning to understand. Now. I'll try and be quick. OK. So this is what Kevin has told me. Adela goes off with Donald after I'd screamed at her. Adela is feeling all rejected, so she lays this self-pity number on Don – everybody hates me, it's because I'm so brilliant, nobody treats me normally, they're scared of my sexuality (I know – as if!). Isn't it awful fancying someone when they don't fancy you etc. etc. And THEN she says – "I know you know how it feels Don, with Duck not fancying you but liking KEVIN instead . . ."'

'I know all this,' I said. 'Adela told me herself. But none of it alters the fact that Don and Adela are now an item. So are you and Kevin.'

'That's only because I put him straight yesterday. I said Adela was just up to her tricks. *You* like Donald.

It was *me* –' here she had the grace to blush – 'who liked him.'

'So what's new? Has Kevin said anything to Donald about me?'

'Well, no, not now he's going out with Adela, but he did tell me that Don *was* mad about you.'

'We have to go back in, don't we?'

'Let's skive off supper. I'll tell Kevin that's what we're doing.'

I still couldn't look at Donald when I went back to my seat. But I had a little spark of hope. It went out, frequently, because then I thought of him and Adela and how it was too late to change anything, but I still felt a bit better. Everyone went to the common room after the rehearsal, but I went back to the dormitories. I didn't want to have to watch Don and Adela, especially now. Jessa came and fetched me. 'I don't want to stay here,' I said. Adela might come in.

'Let's go to the gardens by the music block, then you won't worry about your jazz practice.'

'I'm tempted to miss that.'

'Don't you dare let Kevin down!'

'OK, OK!'

'Right, now, where were we?'

'Kevin knows *you* like him, not me. He also knows that Donald likes me – sorry liked. But Donald doesn't know I like him. In fact, quite the opposite, because Adela had told our Donnie what I told her on Day One – namely, that I don't find him attractive . . . '

'Do you mean – you really said that?'

'On Day One – well, our first whole day – yes.'

'So when did you change your mind?'

'On Day Two!'

'The bit I don't understand is what made Donald get off with Adela. Witchcraft is the only thing I can think of. Something pretty bloody powerful – after all, we know it's you he has the hots for.'

'*Had*. Had the hots for.'

'No. Something happened. Someone did or said something that set it all in motion.'

'Adela didn't like Kevin making up to me, that's for sure.'

'Neither did I!'

'But you're not the vindictive sort, not to me, anyway.'

'And Adela most definitely is. And it's not as if Kevin was faking his interest, unfortunately! I think we're getting somewhere Han.' We heard voices and sounds of furniture being moved in the music room. 'They're setting up. I'll just say hello to my gorgeous Kevin, and then leave you to it.'

Jessa made an entrance. I hung back. The boys were all in there. So was Adela. She was sitting on Don's lap, all over him. Dead sexy. I couldn't look. Jessa was brilliant. 'Come on Adela,' she said. 'These guys have work to do.'

Adela slid reluctantly off Don's lap. 'OK.' She smiled radiantly at Donald. 'Just imagine you're playing to me.' She blew him a kiss and scampered after Jessa, sweet as pie, now they were no longer rivals.

I decided that the best way to handle things was to excuse myself by saying I still felt a bit rough. It wasn't a lie. Rarely in my life have I felt in so much pain. Don was a bit subdued. Worn out, I should imagine. So we had a very workmanlike practice. Technically it was coming on really well.

But then Sam, who doesn't usually say much, spoke up. 'What's happened to you guys? Where's the soul? This is jazz you know. You have to put your heart into it. Tuesday night it was brilliant – loads of heart and soul. Tonight it was crap. What's changed?'

'Did my best,' muttered Kevin.

'Sorry,' Don and I said in unison. I wanted to look at him and get one of those smiles, but I didn't dare. I knew what had changed, even if I didn't understand the whole story.

In the end it was Adela herself who filled me in. Jessa had come in blissfully happy. Kevin was a dream.

Kevin was just so sexy. Kevin couldn't believe why he hadn't got together with her earlier. Her other boyfriend was history. Kevin, Kevin, Kevin. She fell asleep with a sigh. Needless to say, Adela hadn't put in an appearance so far. She turned up half an hour later. I was still tossing and turning, half waiting, I realised, for her to come in from being with Don.

She seemed to know that I was still awake as soon as she saw me. 'Duck!' she hissed. 'It's too early for bed. Come out with me.'

I can't think why I agreed to, but I did. I set off for the lime grove and she danced along beside me in the summer night. 'I wanted Don to stay out all night with me,' she said (Adela didn't know the meaning of the word tact), 'but the old goodie-goodie wanted to go to bed. He's had a hangover all day, as you probably gathered.' (I hadn't.) 'He doesn't seem to be interested in everything that's on offer, if you know what I mean.'

'Perhaps you're rushing him,' I said dully.

'Maybe,' she said. 'But he was happy enough yesterday, *once* I got a bit of alcohol down him. Well, quite a lot of alcohol. I was trying to cheer him up. Bit of a lightweight though. He was nearly puking up all the way home!'

'Probably not used to it.'

'Still, he's cute. I quite like having him around. Especially if Kevin is so determined to be with Jessa. It

125

passes the time, doesn't it?' She tossed her curls and lit a cigarette. 'Thank God this is nearly over. Two more days of prison and then – Italy! Sea, sun and you know what. I can't wait.'

I was gobsmacked. She talked about Don, *my* Don, as a plaything. And a temporary one at that. Did he know?

'I'm going back now,' I said. 'Better if we don't sneak in together. You finish your cigarette.' I didn't trust myself to speak and my brain was reeling.

Thirteen

I couldn't get to sleep. I heard Adela come in, though she slipped into bed like a shadow. All my thoughts were just 'If only . . . ' I went over and over the events of the last few days – after all, I had had *a* relationship with Don, even if it hadn't come to anything. We'd been friends. He'd taught me the saxophone. We'd been stuck in a dark room together for several hours, well two. We'd played in a jazz group. I'd listened to his songs. In fact, the more I considered it, the more I realised that maybe it *had* been leading somewhere. Or it had been until Adela got in on the act.

To be fair, Adela had always liked Donald. And I had told her categorically that *I* didn't fancy him. But then . . . she didn't need Donald. She could have had anyone. Except for Kevin, of course. Jessa and I had been right. If she couldn't toy with Kevin then she was going to toy with Donald instead.

I tossed and turned until my sheet was twisted up like a rope and my duvet had all gathered in one corner. I wanted to be asleep – tomorrow was the last whole day and I had to do something about Donald. There was a complete run-through in the afternoon as well as the usual rehearsals and practices, not to mention the last-night barbecue by the swimming pool . . . But then Donald was going out with Adela. They were a couple. He was probably hopelessly in love with her by now. No wonder. She encouraged him. She made him feel good about himself. She wasn't inhibited. And he'd probably never *really* fancied me. How could you fancy someone called Duck?

I must have fallen asleep eventually, though I know it wasn't until after the dawn chorus. I woke up at the rising buzzer feeling wide awake in a lightheaded kind of way. Jessa and Gemma were stirring. Adela was comatose. I decided to get up quickly, to be ahead of the game.

It was another gorgeous morning. I had a shower and washed my hair and shaved my legs. I was going to be irresistible today. I dried my hair with the hair-drier and dressed in my skinniest top and nicest jeans.

I went over to breakfast with Jessa, secure in the knowledge that Adela wouldn't make it, and headed for the boys' table. 'Hi Kevin! Hi Donald!' Donald gave me one of those anxious grins. I battled on. 'We've got a lot of rehearsing to get in today, guys. How do you propose to squeeze it all in?'

'One after lunch and a quickie before the disco is what I thought,' said Kevin.

Max was smutty as usual. 'And that's just with Jessa.'

Jessa went pink and giggled. 'Oh shut up, Max.'

I had to say something quickly before Max could make any jokes about Donald and Adela. 'OK, I'll be there,' I said, wishing I could think of something amusing to add. But I couldn't. It was hard enough just swallowing my cornflakes.

Jessa rescued me. 'There's quite a bit to do for the disco – apart from praying for the weather to stay nice. The kitchens are providing the food and the Horns are sorting out the sound system but we need to decorate the place a bit. I wanted candles every-where, but we're not allowed. I think I'm going to have to buy fairy lights from a garden centre some-where. You'll drive me, won't you Kevin?'

'Are we going to sneak in any booze?' said Max.

'Last night, and all that. There's not a lot they can do to punish us.'

'I don't really think we want hangovers on the concert day, do we?' said Jessa. 'Anyway, Max. You shouldn't be thinking about booze.'

'Ah, but I do, Jessa,' said Max. 'And all sorts of other things. All the time. You can't imagine the things I think about.'

'I don't think I want to,' said Jessa.

'We know what you think about, Max,' said Kevin. 'Because you talk in your sleep.'

'That's only because *I* don't get the chance to see it in the flesh—' I was beginning to wish I hadn't joined this lot for breakfast. Kevin and Jessa were smiling indulgently at one another and the talk was getting dangerous again. Donald was looking everywhere but at me. It was time to go, but I was proud of myself. I wasn't going to go out of the course with a whimper, oh no.

I stood up. 'See y'all. Jazz practice straight after lunch then. See you two in sectionals. I'm off to practise my piccolo part. Don't want to muck it up.' And I walked out trying not to look self-conscious and willing Donald to be watching me wistfully and hoping I wouldn't hear gales of laughter just as I got out of the door.

I was serious about practising the piccolo. This was for the Rimsky-Korsakov. I'd only realised yesterday just how exposed it was. I couldn't bear the thought of Mum criticising my performance. Actually I couldn't bear the thought of Mum – or even home – at all at that particular point. Despite everything, I didn't want the course to finish. Or at least, not until I'd resolved things with Donald. I tramped up to the music school, my mind whirring as if I'd been wound up. That was it; even if Donald didn't want to hear, I knew I needed to tell him that I had liked him all along and that I did fancy him. If he wanted to be with Adela, well that was fine (well, not really, but that's what I'd say, anyway). I'd just been too shy to let him know how I felt. I suspected that that had been his problem, too, but I don't suppose it was for me to tell him.

I worked hard at the piccolo. It's not really an early-morning instrument, especially if you haven't slept much. But I had such a feeling of time running out that I was prepared to work hard at everything today. I wanted to be perfect in every department. So that if things went wrong they couldn't be blamed on me. I would have liked to have had a bit of a go on the sax. I could have gone and borrowed it, I knew where Don kept it, but I didn't want to delve amongst his things. I was too frightened of what I might find. I decided to ask him for it at the sectional – at least Adela wouldn't be there. And I needed to take full advantage of those times from now on.

We had a five-minute break. Hannah – other Hannah – had nipped out for a drink. Jessa was going over her part with Miss Claggan. There was no one between Donald and me. As if in a farce, we both started speaking at once. 'Hannah—' 'Don—' I pushed on. 'I need a bit more time on the sax – any chance I could borrow it for twenty minutes before the practice?'

'Yes, sure. I'll come up with you after the sectional. Check the reed and stuff.' He looked at me as if he was about to say something else, but I cut in. Hannah was making her way back.

'Thanks.' The sectional was starting again.

Donald waited for me by the door as we came out. Maybe Kevin had said something to him. Jessa gave me a meaningful 'go-for-it' glance as she passed us. Don was looking particularly good today – well-fitting Levis and a top that matched his eyes. We set off up the stairs to the instrument store. Somehow it felt like old times. He found the sax. 'Which practice room are you in?'

'I'll go in the one we use for jazz. I'm skipping lunch.'

'Do you want me to bring you something? You know what happens—' and he gave me one of his dazzling grins – nothing anxious about it. A bubble of relief welled up in me – brought tears to my eyes. I took off my glasses and flicked my hair back. 'Hey Hannah – are you all right?'

'Yeah, yeah,' I laughed, and saw the look of relief on his face.

'I hoped you weren't—'

'No, I was just remembering the embarrassment. I'm fine. Really. Not hungry.'

He turned at the door. 'Hannah – I –' He was at it again.

'Donnie! There you are! Coaching the Duck again are we?' Thanks Adela. She tucked herself under his arm. I wanted to shut my eyes. 'Lunch-time, Donnie lad. I thought I'd come and fetch you.' And she dragged him off. But not before he'd thrown an indecipherable glance in my direction. I gritted my teeth. The day was far from over. I *would* sort it out. I *would*.

Adela came with Donald to the jazz practice. When they arrived her arm was hooked firmly in his. I chose to think that he didn't look very comfortable, but that was probably just because I felt so annoyed. I put the anger into the music and of course it sounded great. We stayed with *Take Five* and *Yesterday*, saving the other two for the evening practice. I caught Donald's eye as he sang the harmonies during *Yesterday* – and he looked away quickly, but I saw a tell-tale flush on his neck that gave me an odd satisfaction. Adela sat swinging her legs throughout and for the first time ever she was full of praise at the end. 'That was amazing,' she said. 'Even you, Duck.'

Don leapt to my defence. 'What do you mean, even Duck? Duck has more soul than the rest of us put together!'

Then Jessa appeared. It was still only two-fifteen. 'Come on, Kevin, we've got to pick up those fairy lights.'

'Oh, OK. Sorry everybody, I forgot. I promised Jessa.'

'What's all this about?' Adela didn't like not knowing what was going on.

'It's for the barbecue disco thing,' said Jessa. 'We want to make the pool look really romantic, so we're hiring fairy lights. It's all sorted, but we've got to pick them up. Kevin's driving me.'

'So you're stopping?' Adela hopped down from her seat. 'Great. Come on, Don, come with me for a fag,' and she tugged at his shirt.

'Hang on a minute.' Don shook her off. 'Not now, Adela. We have to clear up. You go, Kevin.'

'I don't want to clear up. Can't I come with you two, then?' Adela asked Kevin and Jessa.

But Jessa wasn't having any of it. 'We can manage on our own, thanks,' she said. 'We need to hurry, Kev.' They left.

Adela hung around. We were busy tidying up but she didn't offer to help. Then Sam said, 'I need someone to take my double-bass down for the run-through while I put the big amplifier away. Can you give me a hand?' He looked round at Adela who was sitting idly. 'Adela?'

'Oh OK,' she said. 'Meet me in five minutes then, Don.'

Don and I were left alone. I packed up the wind instruments while he sorted out the keyboard and stacked the chairs. He looked at his watch. 'Damn,' he said. 'She'll just have to wait. I said I'd take some chairs down for the run-through.'

I looked at him helplessly. He swept all the music into a pile and stuffed it into the Gap carrier bag he used. He picked up the saxophone case, swung the bag of music over his shoulder and grabbed a stack of three chairs by the backs as he made for the door. 'Sorry about the rush,' he said. 'I thought we'd all have loads of time. Dunno why I agreed to cart chairs around – or go with Adela. Sorry,' he said again.

'It's OK,' I said as, laden, he crashed through the door. I wanted to offer to take the chairs for him, but the words wouldn't come and he seemed intent on punishing himself in this way. Then the Gap bag chose that moment to split open, scattering a snow-storm of sheets of music everywhere. The French windows were open and a wicked summer breeze picked them up and tossed them around.

'Damn,' said Donald again, and worse. I started to chase down the sheets and gather them up as he put down the chairs and the sax to join in. It took us nearly five minutes before we each had a neat sheaf of music. I handed mine to Don and saw a last sheet dancing through the French windows. 'I'll get it,' I said and ran after it, finally stamping it into submission in the courtyard. I bent down to pick it up. It was a piece of handwritten music. I recognised it as one of Don's songs. At the top were three titles, all crossed out. Intrigued, I tried to make them out under the scribble. The first was 'Raindrops On Her Skin'. The second was 'Girl, I Love You' and the third was simply 'Hannah in the Rain'.

I stood, dumbstruck, staring at the sheet of paper in my hand.

I stood there for so long that Don came out to find me. 'Hannah?' he called. 'Where've you got to? Are you OK?' Then he saw me. 'Oh, thanks. It would be such a pain to lose the music at this stage. What was it I was going to have to improvise then?' He held out his hand for the music. I gave it to him. He looked at it, and then at me.

'Oh,' he said.

I didn't move.

'Oh Hannah, I'm so sorry – so sorry – to have embarrassed you. Hannah – are you cross?'

I still couldn't move. He came closer. His face was

bright red – I'd only ever seen it like that a couple of times before.

'*Cross*?' was all I could say.

He held the music close to his chest, as if he couldn't bear it to be seen again. I looked down, shaking my head in disbelief. I wanted to cry. I took my glasses off and rubbed my eyes, but they started to fill with tears.

'Hannah, I'm so sorry,' he said it again. He looked as if he was about to cry too.

'I – I – I wish I'd known then,' I said, looking up at him.

'Nothing's changed, you know,' he said softly, and moved closer to me, towering over me.

I was about to say, 'Yes it has,' but then Adela appeared in person, and made the words unnecessary.

If Adela had seen us moving guiltily apart she didn't comment. '*There* you are, lover!' she shrieked. 'What kept you? I had to have my cigarette all on my own. We'll be late for the run-through!'

For some reason I was less tongue-tied than Donald (nothing to be guilty about, I suppose). 'Don's music bag exploded by the French windows,' I told her. 'Music everywhere. It took us ages to pick it all up. And we've got to take some chairs down. Grab one, can you?'

So we all set off down to the run-through. And I felt

immensely gratified that Adela had her hands full and couldn't paw Donald.

Fourteen

'You're going to have to let Hannah off this jazz practice,' Jessa said to Kevin. She had a firm grip on my wrist. 'She can't possibly play any more or her mouth will drop off. You know she's brilliant. And anyway, I need her for fairy-light duty.'

'What do you think, Don?' Kevin needed back-up.

'Fine,' Don mumbled.

'Great,' said Adela, never far away. 'I'll come up and be your artistic adviser.'

'Whatever,' said Don, not looking in our direction.

Kevin gave Jessa a hug. They were getting *very* married. 'OK, Jess. We'll let her off this time. Just this once, mind . . . Make it look stunning. See you there later.'

I'd been dying to talk to Jessa all through the run-through, but with Don right there, it just hadn't been possible. And it wasn't as if we didn't have plenty to concentrate on. Adela's concerto had been the worst time. She played brilliantly as usual, but Donald hadn't known where to look. Well, down, in fact, but the flush on his neck was a dead give-away.

And Jessa knew none of this. She was prattling on about vegetarian and non-vegetarian barbecues, music for the disco, fairy lights and changing rooms without pausing for breath.

'Jess – hang on,' I said.

'Uh-oh. What's up? You're not going flabby on me are you?'

'No, Jess. Listen. I've got loads to tell you.'

'Tell me while we do stuff,' said Jessa. I obviously looked worried. 'OK. Tell me while we sit down and unravel these lights then.' She put them down on a bench by the pool. 'Fire away.'

So I told her about Don and the song. And how he'd come so close to saying things and doing things, but how Adela seemed to have a sixth sense that brought her on the scene right on cue, every time.

'Blimey, Duck,' said Jessa. 'But what's going to happen? Adela won't let him go, you know. Not without a major struggle.'

I told her what Adela had said the night before. 'It's not as if she really rates him. She was so dismissive, Jessa, so patronising.'

'That's not the point where Adela's concerned. Looks like you'll just have to wait until after the course.'

'*What*? But he really likes me, Jess,' (it felt so

wonderful saying that.) 'He said that nothing had changed. And we've got this whole romantic evening ahead of us.'

'You'll have to fight Adela for him.'

'You didn't have to fight her for Kevin.'

'I almost did. Anyway. Then she had Don.'

'Exactly. What about me in all this? Don't you think I've missed out somewhere?'

'Well, yes. But that doesn't alter the fact that Adela won't just say – Here, take him with my blessing. She's not like that.'

We carried on in silence for a few minutes. 'Maybe you're right,' I said in a small voice. 'Maybe I should wait until she's gone to Italy. It's only the day after tomorrow.' Jessa looked at me sympathetically. 'But it doesn't seem fair. And Jess, I have to have some time with him tonight. We haven't *done* anything yet to – like – ac*know*ledge that we – *lurve* each other.'

'There's always the disco. Tell you what – I'll get Kevin to organise some of the dancing. You know, like a caller. Dance with the girl on your right, or the man opposite you, or whatever. I'm sure Kevin will be only too pleased to oblige. You know how bossy he is!'

'I'm not sure that Adela would go for all that stuff. Don would though.'

Jess climbed a ladder to hook up the lights around the 'dance area' (the patch of grass where we'd been sunbathing). 'Then we'll just get Kevin to be with Adela somehow, even though it will break my heart. The things I do for a friend . . . '

'Thanks, Jess,' I said meekly.

'There. How does it look?' She came down the ladder to admire the thread of lights.

'Not a lot, until we switch them on!'

Jessa bustled over to the power points where the Horns were sorting out the disco. 'Wait for it . . . Ta-da!'

'Wow!' The shadows were long and the August day was already fading. The coloured lights were like fireflies flitting amongst the leaves, or little falling stars.

'Testing . . . 1-2-1-2' Breathy voices imploded over the sound system. The charcoal on the barbecues was glowing and smoke wafted across the pool. Jessa hugged me.

'A Midsummer Night's Dream or what? Bring on Donald! You must be desperate for him. Bring on Kevin, too. I'm certainly desperate for *him*.

'Let's go and get changed,' I said. But all I was thinking was, what on earth would Adela *do*, if she knew I was planning on nicking her boyfriend?

Jessa and I were in the pool when the rest of the jazz band turned up. Adela wasn't with them. I had this on hearsay from Jessa – without my glasses I couldn't see a thing. 'Maybe this is your lucky day after all, Duck,' she said, and hauled herself dripping from the water to throw herself at Kevin. 'Get your kit off, fellas. The water's gorgeous.'

'Mm. *You're* gorgeous,' said Kevin, catching hold of her hand, 'and – aagh – you're all wet!'

'Of course I am! Cheer up, Donald – where's Adela?'

'Oh, cooking up something with Max, I think.' Donald was mumbling again. I couldn't really hear him from where I was in the water, and Kevin and Jessa were squealing.

'What sort of something?' Sam asked.

'Don't ask,' said Donald. 'Hi Duck!' he called in my direction. 'Don't go away, we're coming in.'

Gulp. I nearly drowned at that point. But of course, it was safe for him to be all jolly with me.

Jessa swam up beside me. 'Hey, Duck. They'll be over here soon. Stay cool.'

'I don't feel cool. Anyway, Adela will be here any minute. Probably topless!' I wasn't far wrong. At that moment there was a commotion at the side of the pool. Max was shouting. He sounded hugely over-excited.

'Oi, Don! Don! Don't be a spoilsport! We want Adela to give us an action replay, but she says you wouldn't like it!'

Adela's voice. She sounded hyper, too. 'What do you think Don?'

Don and Kevin were swimming towards us. I didn't dare to look. I felt we were all too naked and vulnerable. Don was saying, 'Help me get out of this one, Kev.'

Then Kevin called, 'Forget it, Adela! Look behind you!'

'Who's there?' I asked Jessa.

Jessa laughed. 'Only the entire staff – in their swimming gear!'

'Woo-oo!' Kevin grabbed me and pulled me under. Don did the same to Jessa. That was all right, somehow. But then Adela was jumping in near us, and I realised that we were all a bit wary of her. 'Hang on in there, Duck,' said Kevin in my ear as Adela popped up beside Don. 'We'll sort you young lovers somehow.'

I stared at him. 'Jess told me,' he said, and dived down to pull her feet from under her. By now the pool was so crowded it didn't matter if you were on your own or not. Adela was pulling Don towards the side. She wasn't being very nice to him – I could hear words like, 'Don't be so *boring*,' and 'It's only a bit of fun.' They climbed out of the pool.

Max was laughing inordinately. He kept shouting, 'I've got a sausage for you, Adela!' and cracking up. I couldn't bear to watch and I couldn't see anyhow, so I stuck with Jessa and Kevin, wishing Don was with me, glad that Adela seemed to be making it easier for him to be with me and faint at the prospect of him really being with me. I wanted him to strike out towards me now and sweep me up in his arms, all dripping water and muscles and cold, firm flesh and warm lips . . .

'Coming in, Duck?' My reverie had stopped me noticing that everyone else was getting out of the pool and heading for the changing rooms.

It wasn't quite warm enough to wander around in a wet bikini, but most of us had sarongs and blouses of one sort and another. It felt a bit odd – but different, anyway, and at least it was warm around the barbecues and the DJ played some boppy numbers to get people going.

'What d'you think?' Jessa was justifiably smug about her efforts.

'Brilliant,' said Kevin, leaning forward as he bit into a burger so it didn't drip down the T-shirt he'd pulled on over his swimming shorts.

Adela and Don were there. 'It's great,' said Adela. 'Especially this fizz!' and she held up her plastic cup in Max's direction. Max responded by raising his cup and hiccupping as he poured in some more Coke from a large plastic bottle.

'Good bottle, this,' he said, unsubtly. 'Duck? Don? Kevin? Jessa? Want some extra-special Coke?'

'Oh, don't bother giving Don any,' said Adela. 'He doesn't approve. I don't expect any of them do. I'll have some more though.'

'You're just mad to be so obvious! All the staff are here, for God's sake!' said Jessa.

'Oh, that's the problem, is it?' said Adela. 'Come on Max, let's go somewhere less obvious then, where all the staff aren't. See you in a bit, guys.' And she ran off after Max, leaving the four of us standing.

'You dancin'?' Kevin asked Jessa.

'You askin'?' laughed Jessa, and they spun off into the dance area.

Don looked nervously in the direction Adela and Max had disappeared in. Then he looked sideways at me.

I looked at my feet.

'Tricky, huh?' he said, to my feet, trying to get me to look up at him.

I did, and wished I hadn't. I wanted him so badly. Still, there was no law against looking at each other. We stood there, gazing into each other's eyes.

He looked down this time. 'I'm scared,' he said. 'I'm scared of Adela, Hannah. I don't know what to do.' He spoke very quietly. 'I'm scared that if we dance together she'll find us. I'm scared that if we disappear off, she'll notice, and find us.'

'Perhaps it should be enough that we know we want to,' I said. 'She's flying off to Italy after the concert tomorrow evening.'

'I can't wait that long,' said Don.

'I'm not sure that I can, either,' I replied.

'Where did she and Max go with their booze, anyway? Good job I'm not the jealous type! Do you think it might be grounds for divorce?'

I couldn't laugh. I was so desperate to be with Don, but he was right – Adela would *know* somehow. And she *was* scary. How would she react? It didn't bear thinking about.

'Let's go and line up for a sausage and stand close to each other . . . ' Don was still capable of making a joke of it. He lowered his voice to a whisper. 'Cheer up, Han. We'll laugh about this one day – won't we?'

'OK,' I said. We got on the end of the queue. Kevin and Jessa jigged along after us and Kevin pushed Don into me with plenty of uproarious laughter.

'Anyone seen Adela?' asked Don innocently as he leant against me.

'I'm here!' God! Adela had materialised from nowhere. 'Babe!' she said, and squeezed up against Don.

'Sausage time!' said Max. 'We require sausages, don't we 'Dela?' Max was talking very loudly.

So was Adela. And her words were slightly slurred. 'No,' she said, pouting. 'Not sausages. Smooching. Come on Donnie babe. Come and dance with me. I missed you.' And she dragged him off.

'Lucky sod,' said Max, still loudly.

'Your time will come, Max,' said Kevin.

'Thought it had,' said Max sulkily. 'I mean, look at her.'

We looked. Adela was draped all over Don as they danced a slow one. I could tell that Don was trying to be as detached as possible. But he wasn't finding it easy.

Max set off towards them. He patted a hip flask under his shirt. 'I'll lure her away,' he said.

Kevin looked at me. 'I don't advise it, mate,' he said. 'But I can't stop you,' he added as Max lurched off.

Jessa looked worried. 'We *ought* to stop him, Kev. Adela's got major stuff to do tomorrow.'

'I can't believe Max has enough there to affect Adela that much,' said Kevin.

'I shouldn't be too sure,' said Jessa. 'I know we've got to get Duck up there with Don, but I don't think this is the way to do it.'

I felt helpless. I started to shiver.

'Think of something, Kev. I'm going to force some hot food into my little friend here. Come on, Duck, we're nearly there. It's nice and warm by the barbecue.'

I suddenly felt sick and miserable. 'It's no good Jessa. Thanks for trying and everything, but I just can't bear to be anywhere near Adela and Don together. Not now. I'm going off for a bit.'

'But Duck – after all our hard work! You can't walk out now, just when the evening's going so well.'

'It's brilliant, Jessa, really it is. But I can't honestly say it's going well for me right now. You must see.'

'Yeah. I do. Poor old thing. It must be ghastly. I wish Don could just tell her it's over. But I don't like to think about what she'd do if he did.'

'My point precisely. We're all scared of her. It's ridiculous, but we are. Especially Don.'

'Must make him feel powerful. Fancy knowing that the whole success of tomorrow's concert is in your hands.'

'What do you mean?'

'Well, if he dumps her tonight she'll probably do something really stupid, like running away. And then she won't be able to lead the orchestra tomorrow, or play her concerto.'

'Thanks for that, Jess. You've just made me realise that it's even more of a nightmare than I thought. I think I'll run away instead. See ya!'

Fifteen

I had to get away before I started crying. I felt so sorry for myself that I knew tears weren't far away. I thought I might just go back to the dormitory, but a part of me thought it would be more romantic to weep somewhere near a bank of scented flowers. After all, Don might just come looking for me . . .

Jasmine grew up the wall of the music block and there was a bench in the corner there. In the dusk the flowers seemed to pulsate with scent and light. I sat on the bench and hugged my knees. It was very peaceful. I could hear the music drifting over from the swimming pool, but it wasn't intrusive. The events of the evening went round and round in my head. Don. Me. Don. Adela. I just had to make it through tomorrow and then I could have Don to myself. Maybe it wouldn't be that hard. I had so much to look forward to.

I calmed down as I sat there, breathing the heady night air. Today was nearly over. I just had to make it through tomorrow . . . make it through tomorrow . . . make it through tomorrow . . .

It was dark in a late-summer, velvety way. I felt light and detached, invisible. Without my glasses I could hear and smell and sense far more than I could see. The music from the disco had slowed down and I could hear people dispersing. Some were in couples – there was laughter and furtive giggles. Two people ran past me, quite close, panting and laughing rather than speaking, the boy chasing the girl – I could hear him shaking a bottle of something ready to squirt at her. They rustled off into the distance and then the water obviously hit her. The squeals of laughter made it clear that it was Adela who had been soaked, and Max who had done the soaking. I pricked up my ears.

'Gotcha!'

'Don't!' shrieked Adela, but she was laughing.

'Now you've got to do it!'

'I don't have to!'

'Yes you do! It was your part of the bargain!'

'Oh no I don't!'

'Give me some of your drink then!'

'OK! OK! Calm down. Follow me. I've got a stash of it. Hang on . . . ' I heard the click and hiss of a cigarette lighter.

'Give me one of those, too.'

'All right, all right.' The lighter flicked on again.

I vaguely made out two little red lights moving away. What I failed to do just then was make the connection – if Adela was with Max then she wasn't with Don. I just felt glad that they weren't intruding on my privacy any longer. I hugged my knees again and allowed the scent of jasmine to beguile my senses.

Down below at the disco another slow number was starting up. The evening was definitely drawing to a close. Suddenly my skin prickled. Someone was walking towards me over the grass. She – or he – must have seen me. Damn.

'Hannah?'

I didn't answer – I didn't want to see anyone.

'Hannah, is that you?' It was Don. He was coming closer. He came over and pulled me to my feet. 'Please?'

We stood close. I put my arms around his neck. He held me round my waist and we swayed to the strains of the music that drifted up from below. He bent his head down, pushed my blouse from my shoulders and kissed my neck, gentle kisses. I breathed in the chlorine smell of his hair. He was kissing my throat and my chin and then, at last, our lips met. At some point he drew breath, only to say 'Hannah,' and stroke my hair from my face before kissing me again.

I started to say, 'What about Adela?' but he put his finger over my lips.

'Shh.'

It's the only time I've ever wanted a disco to go on for ever, but the music came to an end and we couldn't ignore the general hubbub of people leaving and packing up. 'One more,' said Don, 'and then I'd better go down and help Kevin and Jessa.' And before I could add anything, 'Don't ask, OK?' Then he caught me up again and I wasn't able to speak for a good five minutes. I wouldn't have noticed if the whole world had come to watch us.

Don let go of me suddenly. 'Uh-oh,' he said, and then, 'I really hope she didn't see us. I'll run down the long way round. You come down in a bit!' and he was gone, leaving me to peer after a familiar sprite clutching a bottle and staggering back the way she had come.

Adela still hadn't come in by one o'clock. Gemma was asleep, but Jessa and I sat on my bed, wondering what on earth to do. I kept saying, 'Oh God, it's all my fault! If only we'd waited . . . '

'Blast her!' said Jessa uncharacteristically. 'It's her own silly fault. She should never have seduced Don in the first place. She's just *so* desperate for love and attention. Bloody artistic temperament.'

'But what can we do?' I wailed. 'I bet she's done something stupid, and then she won't be able to play tomorrow and the course will have been ruined.'

'No doubt she *has* done something stupid and we'd better find her. But she's tough. We'll make her play tomorrow. I'm sick of her calling the tune. We're all stuck here. We're an orchestra – a team, she can't let us down just because of this.'

Jessa was right, of course. She always was.

'We're going to find her, all of us, and confront her. Me and Kevin, you and Don, and Max.'

'Max?'

'Yeah. She's messed him about too, you know. Well, she's sunk to his juvenile level basically. But he's a nice guy. He likes Adela. She led him on something rotten tonight.'

I couldn't deny that. Max, Kevin and Don. All nice guys. Why wasn't Adela able just to be friends with them? Why did she always want them to fancy her, get off with her? 'OK, Jess. We'd better go and throw stones at their windows or something.'

Jess and I were adept at slipping out unseen these days, but we didn't need to throw stones at windows. As we approached the boys' block we heard the dreadful sound of someone retching. It was Max. Kevin and Don were with him. They weren't being very sympathetic.

'Get on with it, Max,' said Kevin.

'Stick your fingers down your throat!' advised Don.

Max groaned.

'Turn away, Max! We have female visitors,' said Kevin. 'Hi Jessa! What are you two doing here?'

Don put his arm around me.

'Oi!' said Kevin. 'Enough of that. That's what got us into this mess in the first place.'

'Not true,' said Jessa. 'Leave them alone. Adela is to blame for *all* this mess. Not any of us.'

'Do you know where she is, Max?'

Max groaned. 'Snuggled up with a large bottle of vodka somewhere. Cow.'

'You didn't have to drink it, Max,' said Jessa severely.

'I didn't,' said Max. 'I drank the cider. And, er, some of the Hooch. OOOO-er – '

'Face the other way when you vomit, please,' Don reprimanded him. 'The ladies don't want to see your supper.'

'Sausages, I seem to remember,' I said.

'Thank you Hannah,' said Jessa. Max was throwing up again. 'Oh yuk. I can't stay here.'

'I'll stay with him,' said Kevin.

'We'll wait just round the corner . . . ' Don spun me round.

'Oh God, does that mean I have to be with you two lovebirds?'

'Hark at who's talking!' I said.

''Fraid so,' said Don.'

Max was in full flow – so to speak – now.

'Hurry up and get it over with, Max,' we heard Kevin saying.

Max groaned some more. 'Leave me alone.'

'Nope,' said Kevin. 'We need you. Adela has gone missing and we've got to find her and make sure she plays OK tomorrow. It's already quarter to two in the morning. The chamber concert starts in just over twelve hours.'

'She's just drinking somewhere,' said Max. 'She saw Don and Duck snogging and she's upset . . . Ooooooh-er . . . here we go again.'

'I'm not sure I can stand any more of this,' said Jessa. 'Leave him, Kev.'

'No,' said Kev. 'We all need to go together. Come on Max. Mind over matter. Lead us to where Adela is.'

They came round the corner to us. 'Oh no!' said Jess. 'He's got puke all down his T-shirt.'

'Take it off, Max,' said Kevin. 'Can't have you offending my girlfriend.'

'Wear my sweatshirt,' I offered. 'It's not as cold as I thought.' And I had Don to keep me warm.

'Wow,' said Max, as he put it on.

'There, you see? He's cheering up already,' said Don. 'And so he should. Come on.'

'I don't know where she is,' said Max.

'I bet I do.' I felt pretty sure she'd be in the lime grove. Perhaps, like me earlier, she half wanted to be found.

We found her curled up. The bottle was on its side and almost empty. It was hard to tell whether she had passed out or fallen asleep.

'Adela? Wake up!' I rubbed her back tentatively. There was no response.

'Let me try,' said Kevin. He shook her quite roughly by the shoulders. 'Adela! Don't be silly! Wake up and talk to us.'

She emitted a grunt that sounded mostly like 'Go away.'

'We're not going anywhere,' said Kevin. 'Not without you, anyway.'

Another groan. 'I wish I was dead.'

'That's crazy,' said Kevin. 'We'd be bloody cross with you if you were.'

Jessa was whispering. 'She's drunk one hell of a lot. She must be pretty ill. How can we make her be sick?'

Max groaned.

'Just make her smell Max,' said Don. 'He still stinks. He makes me want to throw up.'

'I've got a bottle of mineral water,' said Kevin to Adela. 'Now I want you to sit up and glug some down. Come on, sit up.'

'I want to die,' said Adela. 'Nobody loves me! Don doesn't love me!'

'Cut the drama, Adela,' said Jessa brusquely. 'You don't love Don. Or Kevin or Max. But luckily for you we all like you. Can't think why, but we do. And we want you to feel better.' Adela was slumped against the tree now.

'Oh, the world's going round and round.'

'That's because you're drunk,' said Max. 'You'll feel better when you've been sick.'

'I'm no lightweight!' said Adela furiously, but then she started to retch, too.

'This has been the most disgusting night of my life,' said Jessa. 'You'll have to be sick on your own, Adela. I just wanted to talk to you, not go through all this.'

'Go away then,' said Adela rudely. And then her head fell on her chest again.

'Sit her up again, Kev,' said Jessa sounding anxious. 'She mustn't be allowed to fall asleep if she's going to be sick. People die that way.'

'Jimi Hendrix,' said Max usefully. 'Funnily enough I feel a lot better now. Better out than in, eh? Come on Adela, we're all going to prop you up, and you're going to drink water and vomit for us like a good girl.'

Adela was unwilling. Her head lolled alarmingly. 'This is not good,' said Jessa. 'Maybe it's more than we can cope with. What if she needs a stomach pump?'

'Give it five minutes,' said Don. 'After all, it's only luck – for her – that we even found her. Come on Adela, you're going to lean against me and drink the water Kevin's giving you.'

'And then you can throw up on me,' said Max. 'See? All your favourite men looking after you!'

I was slightly shocked by his frivolity in such a serious situation, but his words had obviously struck a chord.

'Yeah,' said Adela, slurrily. 'That's right. All my favourite fellas. I love you all . . . ' She paused. 'But you don't love me . . . ' and proceeded to throw up all over Max – and *my* sweatshirt.

'Well done,' said Max, unperturbed. 'Actually I *am* pretty crazy about you, Adela, but now isn't really the time to tell you. The important thing is that we are all fond of you and we don't want you to be dead. You muck us about something rotten – ' he paused to think – 'but then you seem to play by different rules from the rest of us.' He took off the offending sweat-shirt and elbowed Don out of the way so that Adela could lean on him. 'But you really shouldn't play games with your friends, Adela. Love and war, and all that, but not with your friends.'

This was turning into quite a speech. Kevin and Jessa were looking on amazed. I realised that Max was definitely saving the day by keeping up the chat, but I found it hard to concentrate because Don was now stroking my ear and cheek with his thumb in a way that no one could see but that I could feel intensely.

'The thing is,' Max continued, 'you might think that we all have ordinary families and boring lives, and you might even envy that, but you've got some-thing that none of us really has – and that is, totally effing superb talent.'

I think we all wanted to say 'Speak for yourself' at that point, but we knew he was right, and anyway, Adela chose that moment to puke again. Max patiently wiped her up with the clean side of my sweatshirt, and carried on as if nothing had hap-pened. 'You see, most people will never treat you as quite normal because you're abnormally brilliant, but it's up to you to choose whether you want that or not. We'll treat you as normal, because we're your regular friends – well, I might not, but this lot will . . . ' He put his arm around her so that her head lolled onto his chest. 'Do you think we can let her go to sleep now?' he asked us.

'Not here,' said Kevin. 'Even if that's what you want, Max! Come on, you two had better get her into bed.'

'But she's revolting,' said Jessa.

'Better than dead,' said Don.

'Marginally,' retorted Jessa. 'Oh all right then. Clean her up as much as you can Max.'

'And then leave that sweatshirt here,' I said. 'I never want to see it again.'

We pulled Adela, grumbling, to her feet. It was a long journey back to the dormitories, but it was so late by then that we weren't too worried about making a noise. We stripped her naked and put her to bed with a large bowl and a mug of water beside her.

'Sleep tight Adela,' said Jessa. 'We'll make sure no one wakes you until lunch time, and then you'd bloomin' well better play your heart out.' But Adela was fast asleep, and soon we were too.

Sixteen

We missed breakfast. Jessa and I managed to roll out of bed for a briefing at half-past ten. Don was looking out for me. I still couldn't believe that we had gone public. He hugged me tight and surreptitiously kissed my hair. Kevin and Jessa smiled on us indulgently. Max looked wan. We told the Goat that Adela had been ill last night, probably something she ate, but that we were confident she'd recover in time for the concerts. The briefing was followed by an hour of last-minute sectionals and then it was really all over bar the concerts. Parents were beginning to draw up in Jeeps and Volvos. Those who had come a long way were scattered across the lawns with picnics. Some were taking younger brothers and sisters for a swim.

Don and I sat together on the bench under the chestnut tree. I couldn't bear the thought of being apart from him for more than a moment. There were five minutes before lunch. It was hard to find time to talk between the kissing, but I managed to ask Don if his parents were coming for the concert. 'Of course,' he said, 'my old man said this morning that he wouldn't miss a jazz concert for anything.'

'Mine will only make it for the evening do,' I told

him. 'They force themselves to come and support me. Makes it easier to send me off on another one.'

Don smiled down at me. I suddenly remembered what he felt about parents, but he didn't preach this time. 'Cynic,' he said. 'They must know they've got one hell of a daughter. Or do they need me to tell them?'

'Don't you dare—' I started to say.

'Oh, aren't you going to introduce me? Ashamed of me already?'

'Don, you know it's not like that! I just couldn't bear it. My mum would be all curious and girlish. And Dad would be embarrassed.'

'Only joking. Anyway, Hannah? Or should I say Duck?—'

'Don't remind me! Though I suppose I don't mind being Donald's Duck . . . '

'I was going to say – this isn't – you know, *it*, is it?'

'What do you mean?'

'We can see each other once we get home?'

I couldn't imagine *not* seeing him. 'Of *course*!' I said. 'We've got the whole holidays ahead haven't we?'

'Not quite,' he said. 'I'm going up to Scotland for three weeks now, but there'll still be some time before term starts.'

'And *after* term starts, I sincerely hope,' I said, 'Or are you planning on cutting a swathe through the sixth form crumpet at Greenwood as soon as you arrive?'

'No,' he said solemnly, 'I'm thinking of starting quite slowly with my year first . . . ' This called for some serious slapping followed by some even more serious snogging.

'Oi, you two, cut that out! You might make me vomit again and it's lunchtime!' My God, it was Adela, and she was laughing.

'Good kisser, isn't he?' she said, and darted off with a Puckish grin. That girl was so unpredictable. One minute trying to drink herself into oblivion and the next minute skipping about like a child. That was probably why she frightened us all so much. But I could have hugged her for taking the awkwardness out of the situation so quickly. We followed her. Don was still a bit embarrassed and fell in with Kev, but I wanted to see how Adela was.

'Adela! Wait! How are you feeling?'

'There's this amazing drug called Alka-Seltzer, Hannah. You take it when you've got a hang-over . . . '

'Are you patronising me . . . ?'

She looked at me without laughing for a moment. 'We're all right, aren't we Hannah? You and me?' She was almost pleading. No apologies or excuses required.

'Sure,' I said, 'we're friends.'

She changed the subject. 'When are your parents coming?'

'After tea,' I said. 'Just for the evening concert.'

'Oh, that's a pity,' she said. 'My mum just rang to say she's coming in time for the chamber concert. And I told her to listen out for the jazz group – since three of my best friends were in it.' Her eyes sparkled, and she added, 'She's been on tour for the last six weeks. I'm really looking forward to seeing her.'

The chamber concert began at four. It was informal and the doors were open onto the gardens. People could come and go between items while the stage was being rearranged. Jessa's wind quintet kicked the thing off in style and Adela's string quartet was programmed to finish it with a flourish. We were second to last – a long time to wait and get nervous. We went off to warm up fifteen minutes early and came on stage to shouts and cheers. My apprehension vanished leaving a simple adrenalin rush. The first two pieces were on the flute – no problem. Then I picked up the sax for *Take Five*. Don smiled at me encouragingly and we took it away. Wow! Did we ever take it away! I don't think I've ever played anything so well in my whole life. It just worked. And when it finished, the audience were on their feet. Kevin had to drown them out on the drums, and then, when they were quiet, we slipped into *Yester-*

day. You could have heard a pin drop. And then the audience went wild! The lads hauled me out in front and Kevin again had to shush everyone while he told them that I had only picked up a sax a few days ago, and added, 'but she had a terrific tutor . . . ' to more catcalls and whistles. I was blushing ferociously, but I have to say it felt good. We filed off and into our seats reserved at the side and prepared ourselves for a classy last act.

Adela led her quartet on to the stage. She looked tiny but completely professional and in control. The wreck of the previous night didn't exist. I heard some loud clapping from behind and caught sight of an elegant blonde woman who looked familiar – of course! – Adela's mother, Celia Barnes. Like Adela she was petite, particularly next to the enormous woman beside her. I'd seen her before, too: Donald's mother in a flowery dress. And then, as I turned back to look at the stage I caught a glimpse of a third woman, face aglow. It was Mum, sitting next to Celia!

The quartet had started. I sat back and watched them play, my hand in Donald's, trying not to be distracted as he stroked patterns on my palm with his fingers.

'Tumultous' was the only way you could describe the applause at the end, 'ecstatic' by the time they had played an encore. The Goat came on stage and thanked us all, saying what a treat the chamber concert was for the staff, particularly as it was all our own work. Then he said that tea was served on the lawn, and that the unfortunate parents who had missed the chamber concert would soon be here for the evening concert which started at seven.

We made our way towards the white-draped tables under the trees. I looked out for Mum, still not quite believing that she was actually there, not sure if I wanted her to see me with Donald.

But she was waiting for me. And something had changed, she looked different. 'Hannah! I wouldn't have missed that for the world!' And she turned to Don as if I had a boy on the end of my arm every day of the week – 'Well done, it was terrific. I just felt so proud of Hannah – and you all . . . '

'Thanks,' said Donald warmly. 'See you later, Han. I'm off to find my folks. Bye Hannah's mum.' And he gave me one of his grins, which *almost* said I told you so. I waited for a comment from Mum, but it never came. She just gave me a hug. I couldn't think why I felt so choked.

'Dad will get here in time for the concert,' she said. 'He'll be really sorry he missed your jazz though, especially when I tell him what a star you were. You know, Hannah, you just looked so at ease and cool up there. I felt quite jealous!' Still nothing about Donald. 'But I had an inkling it was going to be special when Celia Barnes said that Adela's best friends were in the jazz band. And then that lovely motherly Scottish woman told me that the young saxophonist was the one to look out for, and proudly added that she knew because it was *her* son's girlfriend . . . ' Mum smiled at me. 'Don't worry, I kept quiet. I didn't want to embarrass you.'

Well! That was what was different about Mum. She seemed – understanding. We headed for the food and I was spared any introductions by Dad arriving. J was with him, and, funnily enough . . . he looked different too. Maybe he'd had an eventful week as well. 'It's all we heard as we came over here,' said J. ' "Wasn't Hannah brilliant . . . Duck was amazing . . . " So what have we missed? Another piccolo solo?'

'You've still got that to come,' I said.

'You missed an extremely groovy young saxophonist,' said Mum, 'who has only been playing for a few days but who knocked 'em dead.'

My brother looked at me with a certain amount of respect. 'You?'

'So it would seem,' I said smugly.

'Well, I'm sorry I didn't cut work like your mother. I thought your conference went on all afternoon, dear,' said Dad.

I looked at Mum questioningly. 'I don't expect they missed me. I just thought, to hell with it – I want to go and hear Hannah.'

'Mother!'

'I didn't know I was in for quite such a treat, though. Shows the best decisions are always rewarded, huh?'

The concert was, needless to say, a triumph, and Adela's performance was simply breathtaking. I felt euphoric at the way things had turned out, and I think lots of us felt that way. So when the Goat finally bade us farewell at the end of the concert and said he felt it had been a highly successful ten days and that – despite a certain amount of high spirits – the 'children' had all learned about themselves and each other as well as about music, I thought about Adela and about blokes and about love and about unhappiness and about friendship – and felt inclined to agree with him as I joined in the cheering and foot-stamping. Two people were called to the front of the stage for special mention and bouquets: Jessa for organising the last-night disco and Adela for her performance. As they stood there clutching their flowers a strange noise started up in the orchestra. It dawned on me with horrifying certainty that it was a Donald Duck noise. The Goat cleared his throat. 'And each year we also like to pick out a star from the chamber concert. There was no doubt amongst the staff that that honour belongs to Hannah Gross on the saxophone.' Aagh. I squeezed past the other

Hannah and Donald for the last time and staggered to the front. 'Well done – Duck,' said the Goat, and handed me my bouquet.

Donald and I kept our parents waiting for a further ten minutes while we revisited an unlocked practice room for old time's sake. 'I know this is only goodbye for now,' said Don, 'but Han – it's been great, this last bit, hasn't it? This will have to keep us going for the next three weeks.' He pulled me in and leant against the door so no one could disturb us. He was getting a bit carried away when there was a loud knock on the door.

Don looked out sheepishly. It was Kevin and Jessa, also looking somewhat tousled. 'Come on, kids,' said Kevin. 'I've been told to round everyone up. You're not the only ones locked in practice rooms, you know. Let's see who's in here . . . '

He knocked smartly on the next door along. 'Bog-off!' came a familiar voice. Then Adela came out. She wiped her mouth, smiling, but her grin wasn't half as wide as Max's, who stood in the doorway, all signs of wanness long gone, and punched the air.

*Don is the best thing that has happened to me in my life
and I don't want our relationship ever to end. We wrote to
each other all the time he was in Scotland and since he's
got back it's just got better and better. We like doing the
same things. We've been to hear bands and gone swimming at the lido, even wandered around the shopping
mall – but mostly we've just flopped about at each
other's houses. I've now heard the full version of the song
– with the sweetest, most blushmaking words you can
imagine. It's called* Rain on her Face *and it's all about
the time in the music school during our first jazz practice
when I came in from the rain and flicked water all over
him! He said that's when it happened for him . . .
Romantic old thing.*

*I've seen the others a bit, but it's Sophie I'm longing to
tell. She's not coming back until the last minute, so we're
having the sleepover at my house. Mum is cool about that.
She's been amazingly cool about everything. She did say
she was a bit anxious about me being only fourteen and
Don being sixteen, but in fact I'll be fifteen before
Christmas, and Don is one of the youngest in his year.
She also reckons that our generation is about a year ahead
of hers, so she isn't that worried. She let on that she had a*

serious relationship that started when she was fifteen and lasted until she went to university. 'What happened then?' I asked her.

She looked all girlish, remembering. 'He went to university in the States. We were devastated at first, but then we both made new friends, grew apart – and of course we couldn't see each other. He writes to me sometimes, though, even now . . . '

'Mum! I do believe you still have a thing about him! It's OK. I won't tell Dad.'

She laughed, wryly. 'No, it's not like that. Well, not really. But that first great romance is one you never forget. So make the most of it!'

'You bet!'

I had lots of phone conversations with Jessa before she went on holiday with her family, but somehow our age difference seems to matter more away from the course. She also lives too far away for us to meet up without quite a bit of planning. I'll look forward to seeing her next time we play together though.

I've had a couple of postcards from Adela in Italy, mostly listing her latest conquests. I think about her a lot. I've never met anyone as volatile as her before. I looked that word up in the dictionary and it really describes her perfectly: 'capable of readily changing from a solid or liquid form to a vapour . . . liable to sudden, unpredictable or explosive changes . . . ' I don't think I could ever trust her, but I am fond of her. And my lasting impression *of her is as a fey, impish creature, not quite human, and of how, like Puck in* A Midsummer Night's Dream, *she ultimately brought all the lovers together.*

Charlotte turned up first to the sleepover. She looked a bit how I felt – kind of self-satisfied. So I was looking forward to her story.

Mads and Soph arrived together. Soph had literally just got off the boat. She hugged me. 'Like the contact lenses Duck! You look great! I gather there's a lucky guy out there somewhere. Mads told me as we were coming over. She said he was called John – Jonny – or something?'

'Hi Hannah my darling!' Mads wafted in more scented than ever, deeply tanned and immaculately made up. She didn't seem bothered about going in age order this time. In fact I sensed that she was holding back. 'Tell us all about Jonny, Duck,' she said.

'Not Jonny,' I said, and looked at Sophie. 'Donnie. Donald . . . '

'HANNAH!' Sophie squealed. 'Not DORNALD!'

'The very same,' I said. 'But we got him all wrong, Sophie. About as wrong as we could have done.' And I proceeded to tell them about the great guy who was my boyfriend.

Four girls, four lives, one summer.

It was Maddy's idea that all four of them should have holiday romances and report back at the end of the summer.

These are their stories . . .

Sophie

Blonde, drop-dead beautiful Sophie is used to getting her own way, and not worrying about the broken hearts she leaves behind. She's determined that a family camping holiday in France is not going to cramp her style. What's more she knows exactly who she wants . . . but does he feel the same way about her?

Maddy

Finding romance has never been a problem for Maddy – she's always been a beauty and dramatic with it. So she can't wait for her exotic holiday in Barbados with Dad – it's going to be brilliant, and so different from life at home with impoverished Mum. The stage is set – but is romance all that lies in store for Maddy?

Charlotte

Shy, dreamy Charlotte has been going to the Lake District every year for as long as she can remember and she's loved Josh from afar for as long. But this year she's going without her older sister. It might be the chance she's been waiting for. What if Josh notices her – just because she's four years younger than him – it doesn't mean all her dreams won't come true – does it?